Black Assassin

Barbara Kimberly

Copyright © 2024 by Barbara Kimberly

All rights reserved.

No portion of this book may be reproduced in any form without written permission from the publisher or author, except as permitted by U.S. copyright law.

Contents

1. Prologue — 1
2. Chapter 1. — 4
3. Chapter 2. — 14
4. Chaper 3. — 24
5. Chapter 4. — 36
6. Chapter 5. — 48
7. Chapter 6 — 67
8. Chapter 7. — 78
9. Chapter 8. — 83
10. Chapter 9 (Explicit) — 93
11. Chapter 10. — 103
12. Chapter 11. — 111
13. Chapter 12. — 117
14. Chapter 13. — 124
15. Chapter 14. — 131

16. Chapter 15. 137

17. Chapter 16. 144

18. Chapter 17. 149

19. Chapter 18. 156

20. Chapter 19. 163

21. Chapter 20. 170

22. Chapter 21 177

23. Chapter 22. 185

24. Chapter 23. 195

25. Chapter 24. 201

26. Chapter 25. 207

27. Chapter 26. 216

28. Chapter 27 223

29. Chapter 28. 229

30. Chapter 29 235

31. Chapter 30. 242

32. Chapter 31. 248

Prologue

I positioned myself behind a tree, waiting for the right signal. It was a dark night, not even the moon's shimmering gleam was shining in the sky.

A perfect night for assassination.

I heard a bird chirping in the distance but I knew it wasn't a bird, it was Eva giving me the signal. I nodded my head up in the tree and stepped from behind my hiding spot. I noticed a wolf on guard with its back facing, unaware of his surroundings.

Thank Goddess I disguised my scent or else I would have been given away instantly. I took out my knife hidden within my combat boots and waved my handover it. It instantly grew into a sword with the word Alituum (winged creature) inscribed into the blade. I quietly crept up behind the wolf and stuck my sword into its back, reaching forward to hold its mouth shut so it would make no sound. Once it fell motionless to the ground I prayed over its unmoving corpse 'ut inveniam luna dea est anima tua' (May your soul find Moon Goddess).

I chirped up to the tree next to me and watched as a figure climbed out of the tree and nod towards me. I advanced into the pack territory without a sound to my footsteps. There weren't many guard wolves out tonight which meant less blood shed tonight.

We advanced toward the pack house. I looked up at the three story house and then looked back at Eva. She held three fingers up and I nodded, I noticed a balcony on the side. That had to be the Alpha and Luna's because no other room had a balcony attached to it. I jumped up and landed quietly on the balcony.

You may ask how did I jump all the way up to a three story balcony from the ground, well it's just the perks of being an Angel.

I slid the sliding doors open since someone foolishly forgot to lock it and I quietly walked in.

The Alpha and Luna were both silently sleeping on their bed and I walked over to the Alpha first so I can take him out. He was a handsome Alpha, too bad he was a murderer that needed to be destroyed.

I raised my sword above his chest and then plunged it into his chest. His eyes shot open as the celestial silver pierced his heart. I looked into his eyes with no emotion and I watched as the life escaped his eyes.

I quickly walked over to the Luna. She sat up, about to cry out in pain due to the ache in her chest but I had already plunged my sword into her heart. She looked up into my blue eyes with despair and fear. I noticed she looked over at the other side of the room and my eyes followed what she was staring at and I noticed a crib.

I took my sword out of her now lifeless body and walked over to the crib but as I raised my sword something made me do something I have never done before.

I hesitated.

What I saw in the crib was a small red head sleeping child. I sniffed the air and noticed that this child was developing a smell.

A metallic smell.

This child was a vampire and it had to be about 2 years old. I minimized my sword into a knife and stuffed it back in my boot. I carefully picked up the child and held it in my arms. I swiftly walked to balcony and jumped down landing smoothly onto the ground.

"What is that Ava?" Eva hissed.

"This is not their child, they must have kidnapped it or something," I said.

"Explain when we get back," Was all she said.

I felt the bones in my back begin to rearrange and something shooting out of my skin. My wings shot out of my back as I stretched them. Eva and I took off into the night sky with the child still safely in my arms.

Another name off my list.

●●●●●●●●●●●●●●●●●●●●●●●●●●●●●●●●●●●●●●●

Chapter 1.

"You know people could mistake you for having bipolar disorder," Eva said as she sat up in a tree staring down at Ava.

I raised a brow. "Why would someone think that?"

"Well..." She said as she hung upside down from the tree branch.

"When we have a mission to do your personality and demeanor becomes cold and soulless and you got that 'I don't give a shit about anything' attitude. But on a normal day you're all happy and annoying and stuff," She said as she swung back and forth.

Evangeline was my fraternal twin sister from our mortal days on Earth to now as we are Angels, that was all we were ever truly allowed to know of our past mortals lives and even then that was pushing it. We are Angels, the children of the Moon Goddess who aid in her wishes and commands and play out our assigned roles in her divine world.

Every Angel had a role they were responsible for, whether it were to guard the Divine Moon Goddess herself, protect humans or werewolves, guard the Underworld or the gates of Sanctity but in this case mine was to assassinate.

Sometimes the Moon Goddess's creations were morally unfit to continue living in her mortal realm and I amongst may others were given the responsibility of releasing their souls so that they may go through judgement.

I assassinate bad people.

Amongst us there were 5 assassin Angels and I was the highest rank of them all, that's how I got my black wings. i was trained to kill with no mercy and harbor no hate in my heart.

"Ava! Eva!" We both heard a scream. I stood up and brushed the dirt off myself as Eva jumped out of the tree as we rushed to the sound if the scream.

There, crouched a small red head in the bushes with extremely pale skin and beautiful green eyes.

"Elizabeth what are you doing?" I hissed.

"All of a sudden there came a large growl from behind me as both Eva and I froze. We slowly turned around and was greeted by a grey rogue wolf baring its canines at us, ready to pounce on us at any moment. I stepped forward as I held my hands up, trying to show that I was not a threat.

"Rogue we mean no trouble, turn back to where you came from and we won't harm you," I warned.

It stamped its paw into the ground with aggravation dancing in its eyes as it growled and began charging at us. In a flash I pulled my knife out of my boot and watched as it grew into a full sword just as the wolf pounced on top of me, plunging itself onto my sword as it pierced its heart. I laid there with a now bleeding wolf on top of me with a sword plunged into its heart.

Not something I was a fan of.

I pushed the lifeless beast off me and dusted my self off, getting up from the ground.

Avangeline, are you alright?" Eva asked as she stood next to me.

"Don't ever call me that, but yes I am fine," I slightly hissed as I minimized my sword and stuff it back into my boot, hidden from anyone's gaze except my own.

I trudged back over to the bushes where I plucked out the small redhead and held her in my arms as we made our way back to the camp site.

"I told you to stay near the camp," I scowled her.

"I'm sorry Ava," She said as she buried her face into the pit of my shoulder and I smiled, I just couldn't find it in me to stay mad at her. She was just too adorable.

Elizabeth was the same stolen child I saved from that pack 6 months ago, she was a small baby at the time but due to vampire genes and their rapid growth through a certain time period she was now about 7 in human years.

Once we reached the campsite I noticed Eve standing in the middle of the clearing as she looked up into the sky, her pupils glittering a beautiful gold as she continued to stare up at the sun, a slight tear shedding from her eyes. This was the way our Divine Moon Goddess chose to communicate with us Angels, speaking through our minds and appearing as an image we deep desired. That was one of the ultimate powers of the Divine herself.

Eva lowered her head as she blinked multiple times, her eyes slowly reverting back to their original color as she looked over as me and beckoned for me to come closer.

"The Moon Goddess has granted a mission for us but it's too dangerous for the child to tag along," She said as she motioned towards the child Elizabeth.

"Then we can just take her to the white wolves, no big deal," I said nonchalantly as I shrugged my shoulders.

"Our mission starts there anyway," Was all she said before her large silky white wings painfully sprouted from out of her back and she took off flying into the sky.

I sighed.

I looked up into the sky and noticed it was a dark and cloudy day which meant not as many of the sun's harmful rays shone through the clouds so I could carry Elizabeth without such a big fear that she could get burned. I felt the bones inside of my body twisting and arranging painfully throughout my back, a pain that no longer fazes me and sure enough my pure midnight black sprouted from my skin as I ruffled them in satisfaction, the shine from each feather reflecting from the very little light poking through the clouds. Amongst all the ranked assassin Angels, my wings were the biggest due to my status. To other known mythical creatures I was only a legend that people whispered about, I was an idol only the most powerful dreamed to meet.

I grabbed a hold of Elizabeth as I held her in my arms tightly, securing her so she wouldn't fall.

"Hold on little one," I said calmly before taking off into the sky.

It felt so freeing, having the wind blowing into my curly jet black hair, to zoom past the green tree tops and to just have the entire world right under you. Flying always made me feel free like there were no worries in the world.

I looked down at Elizabeth to make sure she was alright in my arms, I made sure to fly below the clouds so they could shield her from the sun's harmful rays. By foot it would have taken about a day to get to the white wolves pack from where we were temporarily located but by flying it would simply take a couple hours.

"Who is the target?" I asked Eva as I flew up right next to her.

"There is an Alpha in the northern region who managed to capture a white wolf and he plans to use dark magic to take her rare wolf spirit and use it as his own," She shouted as the wind began pounding into our ears from our speed.

I shook my head, trying to imagine what malicious Alpha would do such a thing to his own kind?

A monster that needed to be destroyed.

"Which Alpha is it?" I asked.

"Alpha Jason,"

Evangeline was always sympathetic when it came to taking the life of a werewolf, especially Alpha's, she was never fond of doing it herself but I on the other hand did not care whose chest I was driving my sword into. I never had good experiences with Alpha's, especially not since.....him.

I looked down to analyze my surroundings and realized we were drawing closer and closer to the white wolf pack.

"Ava do the thing!" Elizabeth squealed as she began to wiggle in my grasp. I looked over at Eve as she smiled and immediately dove down under me.

I wrapped my wings around both Elizabeth and I as we began falling out of the sky, spiraling our way down to the Earth.

Elizabeth squealed with joy and just as I knew Eve was right below me I opened my wings like a parachute, ignoring the sheer pain to my wings due to the sudden force of the wind and resistance of my wings, and let Elizabeth fall. I hovered in the air for a moment as I watched the small red head squeal for joy as she flapped her arms almost as if she had wings of her own.

Eve, now her back facing the ground and her arms outstretched for Elizabeth to fall in them, she caught her and wrapped her beautiful white wings around them both and began falling to the ground.

I dove down as fast as I could like a speeding bullet and landed on the ground creating a huge crater from the impact. Eve outstretched her wings let go of Elizabeth, I watched as she fell right into my arms, still squealing with joy.

"Let's do it again!" She laughed.

"Maybe later little one," I chuckled.

She pouted as I gently placed her on the ground.

"Must you always play with my emotions Ava?" I heard his all too familiar deep voice from behind me.

I turned around to see a tall man with long blonder hair up in a pony tail standing behind me with a large grin on his face.

"What did I do Nicholas?" I asked, mocking him.

He stepped forward so that I was now able to see him more clearly. His blue eyes seemed slightly saddened behind that cheerful smile, his skin seemed more dull and tired.

This wasn't the Alpha Nicholas I was used to seeing.

"I hate when you play that game with the kid, I'm always terrified that you're not going to catch her," He said seriously, his smile immediately dropping.

I slapped his arm and rolled my eyes.

"Oh lighten up you big baby, I'm the black winged Angel, I always catch her,"

He smiled once more as he wrapped his arms around my waist, I came in reciprocating the hug. Instinctively my wings wrapped around Nicholas and I bringing us much closer together. It was warm and inviting within this hug, it was almost as if I never wanted to leave.

I unwrapped my wings and lightly blushed.

"Sorry it's an instinct," I muttered as I looked away.

He simply smirked and looked down at Elizabeth.

"Hello little red, did you miss me?" He grinned down at her.

"Did you see me, I was flying!" She squealed as she bounced up and down.

Eve finally landed as she walked over to us, taking Eliza's small hand into hers.

"Come on Eliza, let's take you to see Bethany," Eve said.

She nodded her head as she skipped next to Eve on their way to the pack house.

Nicholas finally turned back to me and sighed, the exhausted look on his face beginning to show more clearly.

"I'm guessing you heard about Lucie getting kidnapped?" He asked.

I nodded.

Lucie was Nicholas's younger sister and one of 12 pack members. Nicholas was Alpha of the white wolf pack, since white wolves were extremely rare and closest to the Moon Goddess than all the other wolves, he was sworn to protect the entire pack with his last dying breath.

"Come on," He beckoned for me to follow him towards the pack house.

We stepped into the grand building that was their pack house, built just big enough for around 20 people to comfortably live. As we walked through the house we ended up in his office which seemed destroyed. Broken bookshelf, holes plastered all throughout the walls, papers everywhere and his broken computer.

He collapsed in his chair as he let out a tired sigh, rubbing his hands against his face.

"Ava, your wings," He said, pointing behind me.

I looked behind me and noticed my wings folded neatly behind me.

"Sorry," I said as my bones shifted, my wings disappearing from sight. I took a seat in the only seat that wasn't broken.

"Alright down to business...woah," Eve said as she peered into the room.

"Yeah, when I found out that Lucie was kidnapped I just couldn't control myself. I desperately need you guys to find her and bring her back safely," Nick pleaded.

Eve simply nodded and left leaving Nicholas and I alone. I stood up and went to sit on Nicholas's lap. He wasn't my mate or my boyfriend but we once were in an intimate relationship. He was there for me when I was going through a rough patch and he didn't even know it. When I was torn down and my confidence destroyed all by that one person.

He was there for me when I was most unstable but in the end we agreed we could no longer be together, he was a wolf and I was an Angel who would be gone for months at a time. It would be most unfair to his mate most of all.

That didn't stop the feelings that we had for each other even though we both knew it wouldn't end well. I rested my head on his shoulder as he sighed.

"I really need you to find her Avangeline," He said quietly.

I slightly flinched at my name and cringed my nose.

"I will find her and I will kill the bastard that took her, after all I cannot fail a mission," I said angrily.

He planted a small kiss on my cheek as he whispered "Thank you," into my ear.

I got up from his lap and smiled as I left his office and walked outside.

As I walked out of the door I heard a scream from behind me and a sharp pain in my back.

"Evangeline I'm going to murder you!" I shouted angrily as she ran off giggling.

"I like to see you try!" She shouted back.

I reached behind me and pulled the knife out of my back that she stuck in there without flinching as I instantly healed. One benefit of being an Angel was instant regeneration no matter the injury.

I stood there as I closed my eyes and imagined a silver bow in my hands. I felt the cold metal materialize in my hand and smirked. My mind itself was like a weapons room, allowing me to store all of my weapons except for my sword so that they were always at my disposal.

I placed an arrow into the bow as I raised it, aiming directly for Eve. I let go and watched as the arrow whizzed straight into her right leg, causing her to fall forward cursing. I ran up to her and watched as she angrily pulled the arrow from out of her leg.

"What the fuck was that for?" She asked angrily.

I rolled my eyes. "You call me bipolar, you're the one that started it," She stood up as she slightly shook her leg and turned away.

"Whatever," She muttered.

Chapter 2.

"You look like an idiot, why is your hair purple?" I scowled at Eve as she strutted out of the pack house. Eve had the ability to change her physical features as a disguise, one of the special abilities the Celestial Being herself granted her for being an Assassin. Even though we were fraternal twins we very much favored each other.

Eve was always the one to have her curly hair in different colors to help everyone figure out which one of us was which and right now it was purple.

"Don't hate on my style, just shut up and come on," she muttered before immediately taking off into the sky, her white wings reflecting in the sun.

I turned back to the house and noticed Nicholas and Elizabeth standing on the porch waving at me. I waved back before turning away and taking off into the sky behind Eve. I spiraled up into the air until I was flying right next to Eve.

Now wasn't the time for fun and games, we had a divine order that needed to be fulfilled.

"See if you can locate Alpha Jason with your vision," Eve instructed.

I nodded my head and closed my eyes as I concentrated hard, trying to focus my energy and power towards Alpha Jason and his thoughts. One of my special abilities granted to me amongst many other abilities was the power to read ones thoughts throughout and locate anyone in this world. No one could hide from me, no one could hide their thoughts from me no matter where they were.

Alpha's and Luna's were a bit more difficult to track and read but not impossible. I concentrated long and hard until I was able to hear something that was associated with Alpha Jason.

'Detaching a white wolf's spirit from her body, something I've always wanted to do but the white wolves have been heavily guarded by the Moon Goddess herself. I can't wait to finally meet and praise the Alpha who successfully captured one,'

I selected my target as that voice in my head, focusing on their thoughts and words. I opened my eyes and noticed a gold trail in the sky that only I could see, guiding me towards my target of choice. I made no hesitation to follow it and I dove down close to the tree tops, the leaving barely touching my underside. I blocked all distractions from my mind including my own thoughts, making sure to never lose sight of the trail. I slowed my speed as I quietly landed on a tree branch, watching a bright gold figure walk in the clearing.

My target.

I blinked twice to return my vision back to normal and looked over to see Eve squatting down right next to me, her wings no longer in sight.

"I couldn't find the Alpha but I was able to find the witch he summoned to help him with the ritual," I motioned towards the figure walking.

Eve nodded and swooped down silently as she tackled the witch from behind, pulling a knife out and holding it against her throat. I jumped down and landed in the shade so that I was careful not to be seen.

"How dare you attack me!" The witch screeched as she clawed against Eve's arm.

"Hold still witch so I'll make sure not to spill your blood on me," Eve spat.

"A divine Angel huh? What have I done wrong now?" The witch smirked.

"Why are you on your way to meet Alpha Jason?" Eve hissed.

"I don't know who you're talking about," the witch said.

'I haven't spoken to a soul about my plans, how does she know of my meeting with Alpha Jason?' I read into the witch's mind. I stayed in the shadows because very few have heard of the true power of the black winged Angel, I couldn't allow for the witch to know of my presence and block me from her thoughts because as of right now I was merely a myth.

"What do you know of separating the wolf spirit from its human vessel?" Eve asked.

The witch froze as she said nothing from her mouth but her mind did all of the talking.

'How does she know my plans? Where is she getting her information from?'

"Normally when a person is mentioned then their face pops into the person mind meaning she has never met Alpha Jason so we can use that to our advantage. Unfortunately she has found a successful way to separate the two so she must die right now," I said as I stepped out of the shadows.

The witch looked over at me with wide pitch blacked out eyes.

"So the legends spoken are true! A black winged Angel does exist!" She screeched out as she tried to fight against Evangeline's grip.

I nodded to Eve and placed my hands behind my back as I watched Eva nod and slit the witch's throat instantly. She fell back on the ground, blood gushing from her neck but of course she would be able to live through this using dark magic. I grabbed my knife from my boot and maximized to a sword and swiftly sliced her head off clean. I picked it up by the hair to examine it and tossed it to Eve.

"Burn it," I hissed coldly as I began walking in the direction the witch was going, when I peered into her mind I was able to grab the directions towards the pack.

My wings shifted back into my back, hidden from sight as I continued walking straight on and curious as to what lies ahead of me. About 20 minutes later I must have stepped over the territory line and into the pack because immediately I was surrounded by wolves. I raised my hands up innocently to show my surrendering. One wolf walked behind a tree and soon enough came back in his human form with nothing but shorts covering him.

"Who are you and why are you trespassing on our land?" He boomed out loud.

"Your Alpha called for me to use my dark magic," I stated.

"You're the witch?" He asked in disbelief.

"Yes I am, hard to believe?" I smirked.

He looked me up and down for a moment, his eyes roaming my body, excitedly looking at my clothing hungrily making me want to shove my knife down his throat but I refrained from doing so.

"Follow me," He said while smirking.

If only such an attractive wolf wasn't a part of such a monstrous pack. He had light honey brown hair with dark brown eyes and darker tanned skin. Sweat glistened from his toned chest and defined abs, shining in the sun.

"Checking me out witch?" I looked up to see the wolf looking back at me and smirking.

I internally gagged to myself even though I was doing just that thing.

"In your dreams wolf," I rolled my eyes, focusing on the mission.

"I always heard rumors that witches were ugly looking beings, always living in the shadows so much their skin grew pale and fragile," He explained.

"I'm not here to make conversation with you, take me to your Alpha," I hissed.

"Maybe when you're done with the Alpha you could come visit me for some fun," He wiggled his eyebrows in her direction. A small silver dagger into my hand, he was wasting my time and getting in my way.

I heard a growl ahead of us both. I looked up to see a tall intimidating figure standing in front of us, he loomed over us with angry eyes, staring deeply at me. The wolf next to me quickly bowed his head.

"Alpha Jason," He muttered.

I whisked away the dagger and stared back into his fierce brown eyes.

"Beta Jonathan who is this?" He spat in my direction.

I repulsed as I felt clearly offended, how dare he spit at me. He wasn't aware of who I was and what I was capable of.

"It's the witch you summoned for Alpha," Jon said, still bowing.

I forced myself to bow to this man to show respect but I bowed to no one except my Moon Goddess.

"Yes my A-Alpha," I gritted my teeth.

"What a beautiful woman, I expected a vile woman," He said with no hesitation.

"Flattery isn't what will get this started," I said impatiently.

He nodded his head and led me towards the pack house. It may not have been as grand as Nicholas's house but it was definitely bigger. The difference was that there were nothing but drunken men surrounding the house shouting obnoxious profanities, fighting each other, completely ignoring those around them.

As I walked by the group with the Alpha, a group of them wolf whistled as they yelled promiscuous things. I felt a dirty hand grope my back side as I immediately turned around to punch the intruder straight in the jaw. He was sent flying away as he held his face in pain, complaining about a broken jaw.

Slapping was for the weak.

I turned back around to see the Alpha smirking at me as his eyes roamed me up and down.

"Impressive," Was all he said.

He led me deeper into the pack house, into the shadows until we reached the end of a hallway where there was a locked door. He pulled out a key and unlocked the door, leading me down deeper into the basement.

"After you," He grinned.

I walked into the dark room that was dimly lit. As I reached the bottom I felt the Alpha's rough hand grip mine and led me to the farthest cell.

He opened it and I noticed a petite figure chained to the wall but I immediately recognized it as Lucie. She looked up to the sound with fear laced in her expression but the moment her eyes landed on me she relaxed a little.

I concentrated hard as I looked into her mind to send her a message.

'Lucie don't be alarmed, I've come to get you out of here and I damn sure will,'

The moment she received the message, relief washed over her entire body.

I felt his rough hands grab me and push me onto the wall rather aggressively.

'What are you doing?" I said coldly as I looked away from him in disgust.

"How can I control myself when you're so beautiful? You're nothing like how I expected you to be, why don't we let the white wolf watch us before we steal her spirit," He said huskily as his eyes began turning a darker shade.

Fine, I'll play along with his little games to make my move. I smirked as I ran my fingers down his face, he immediately took that as a sign and crashed his lips onto mine causing me to fight the urge to gag. The kiss was wet and sloppy, filled with hunger. He quickly broke away to begin trailing kisses down my neck. I reached my hand towards my pants waist where I had my sword hidden, luckily something within me told me to hide it there for the time being. Carefully so he wouldn't notice I reached up behind him and maximized the knife, letting it slice through both him and I.

He gasped as he looked down at the sword in both our chests and smirked.

Now it was my turn to smirk. I turned us around so that his back was against the wall and pushed myself away from him, the sword sliding out of my chest and instantly healing. He slid down to the ground, my weight no longer supporting him, his mouth hanging wide open with shock before finally becoming deceased.

I pulled the sword from out of his back and ran up to Lucie where I grabbed the chains from around her and yanked them off. I slowly untied the rope from her mouth and let her weak body fall into my arms. She looked up at me and smirked.

"Stop trying to play that off, you know that sword in the chest hurt," She said.

"Yeah it hurt like a bitch," I whined as she laughed.

We walked out of the cellar, up towards the stairs where I quietly tried to open the door but it wouldn't budge.

"Shit!" I yelled.

I had to break down the door, wolf strength was no match for an Angel.

I kicked the door and it was sent flying into the opposite wall causing a loud boom throughout the house.

I grabbed Lucie and began running through the house, my wings shifting painfully from my back to make a quick escape. As soon as we reached the front entrance I stopped.

"Lucie grab onto my neck and wrap your legs around my waist," I ordered.

She blushed but did what she was told, I heard the thunderous sounds of footsteps all around me and I knew I had to hurry. Once I knew she was secure I ran out of the door, my wings shielding us as we broke through the door and noticed a group of men around us, staring long and hard at the sight before them.

"STOP HER SHE KILLED THE ALPHA!" I heard a roar from the inside. I instantly took off into the sky, leaving the wolves on the ground to stare up at the sky, trying to comprehend what they just saw. I smirked and continued onward to the direction of the white wolf pack.

I connected to Eve and told her to get back to the pack house.

About an hour later of flying we finally reached the white wolf territory. I steadied myself as I tried to land as smoothly as possible but stumbled along the way.

Landings were never my strong suit.

The moment we touched the ground Lucie let go and attacked me into a bear hug.

"Thank you so much Avangeline!" She screeched out.

I tried so hard not to wince at the sound of my name but it was nearly unbearable.

"You're welcome Lucie, try to be careful next time, I won't always be there to save you," I told her.

I looked behind me and noticed Eve standing there, staring up at the sky with golden glowing eyes, communicating with the Moon Goddess.

I turned back and noticed Nicholas running towards us.

Lucie let go and ran towards her brother, both their blonde hair bouncing in the wind, as Nicholas engulfed her in a hug he looked at her face and growled as he saw the bruises and scratches.

He looked up at me as I shook my head, signaling that the Alpha was no more. His face relaxed as he smiled.

I turned back to my sister Eve as she walked towards me with a serious expression.

"Evangeline are you alright?" I asked worriedly.

She shook her head as she turned to me.

"Our next mission is split up," She said as she gulped.

I laughed.

"Oh come on Eve, you don't like being separated?"

She looked me dead in the eyes as she spoke her next words.

"Your next target is Alpha Derek of the Blood moon pack,"

Chaper 3.

"Alpha Derek is one of the most dangerous Alpha's of the deadliest and merciless Alpha's of the Northern region, he's worse than Alpha Jason," Nicholas stated as we both sat in his office while I stared up at the ceiling, thinking about how I would go on about my next mission.

"And I am one of the most deadliest creatures in the world, you think a simple Alpha is going to scare me?" I said finally turning my head to his direction.

"Well no not scare but definitely put up more of a fight than you are used to, even us white wolves fear him. His methods of torture are inhuman and he kills with no mercy and he destroys packs for the fun of it-"

I cut him off at the end of his sentence.

"He's not as dangerous as me plus that gives me all the more reason to eliminate him from this world," I hissed as I stood up, glaring over at Nicholas.

Just then Eve burst into the room and shook her head as she walked towards me.

"Your target is not to be eliminated, it's more of a secret co-op mission where you need to find some intel but in no means are you allowed to assassinate him," Eve instructed me.

"You'll need a cover story then if you're going to go undercover," Nicholas interjected.

"I am the highest ranking Assassin Angel not some under cover agent, he needed to be eliminated long ago and now you're telling me that the Moon Goddess is telling me not to?!" I looked at Eve with confusion.

It's rumored that he has a secret weapon that he plans on using to start a war, you would think the Moon Goddess would know all of this anyway but it seems as though this is something that you need to learn for yourself without her telling so looks like you'll have to put on your best acting skills," She explained.

What I would have done to switch places with Eve in this moment, she was given the task to disguise herself as a vampire so that she could take out the dangerous clan leader of a coven, something so quick and simple that I could have done but instead I was given a mission that didn't even involve assassination.

"Fine then, what's my cover for this mission?" I asked as I crossed my arms over my chest.

"What about an omega from a recently destroyed pack, that will explain why you don't have a normal scent like a werewolf, human mother and werewolf father," Nicholas suggested.

"I absolutely fucking hate this, how the fuck am I supposed to conceal the real me? I am one of the most powerful beings on this planet and now you're expecting me to bow down to an Alpha?!" I spat the word Alpha.

Never again did I want to feel weak against another Alpha, never again did I want to be manipulated into thinking that I was anything less than what I was.

No man nor Alpha shall hold that power over me ever again.

"Avangeline calm down, it's not that serious," Eve shouted.

I turned to her with a furious expression written all over my face.

"It is that serious and if someone fucking calls me that one more time I'll cut your tongue out of your fucking mouth," I stormed out of the office and out of the house. I outstretched my wings and took off into the pinkish orange sky of the setting sun.

I didn't want to be bothered, I just wanted to be alone for a moment to collect myself. Nothing should be able to trigger me this much, I've seen so many things, so much blood has stained my hands and yet I was so bothered by some simple Alpha. I had a feeling and I just couldn't shake it away.

Was there something more to this?

I landed in the highest tree I could find and looked up into the beautiful sky. The clouds gently floated against the orange pinkish glow, it was like a painting before me.

I watched as a pair of snow white wings circled around the sky, I outstretched my midnight black wings signaling where my location was. I watched as Eve swooped under me and landed on a branch right below.

"What's going on Ava, what was that all about?" Eve asked calmly.

"Hearing my full name gives me pains, I can't describe it or understand why but my body reacts so abnormally when I hear it," I sighed.

"What about you freaking out because of this Alpha Derek?" She questioned.

"You know my past with Alpha's you know what I went through with Liam when I was the lowest ranking assassin Angel, no matter how much confidence I have I can never forget all that he did to me," I said as I blinked, trying to hold back the tears.

"But you are no longer the lowest ranking Angel, you are Ava the one and only Black winged Assassin, you are a myth and legend to all mortals, Liam is gone and he can never hurt you again," Eve comforted as she encouraged me.

I'm a fucking Angel.

"Yeah you're right I'm being dramatic and overreacting, this mission is only temporary and for the Divine Goddess I'll do anything," I smiled.

"You can do it big sis, I know you can," She said.

I looked down at her and smirked.

"It's about time you finally recognize me as the older twin," I grinned before taking off into the sky.

Eve managed to catch up to me and fly right next to me as she shot a glare in my direction.

"That was a once in a lifetime thing that I only do when you might possibly die but of course you won't die no matter how many times I stab you," She laughed.

It was now my turn to glare in her direction. I decided to slap her with my wing before winking at her and diving down as I heard her audible gasp.

Her flight skills were no match for mine.

***

I gave Nicholas a warm hug as my giant wings wrapped around him once more, bringing us even more closer together.

"Gonna miss seeing your face Nicholas," I said as I pouted.

"Same here Ava, except it will be me missing you though," He blushed as he quickly looked down, avoiding my gaze.

I giggled.

"You're so adorable, when the Moon Goddess cursed me with a mate why couldn't it have been you instead of him?" I asked sadly.

He cupped my cheek with his hand and smiled at me with a comforting warmth to his smile.

"Don't think about that right now," He smiled before before planting a kiss on my cheek.

"You should already know what to feed Elizabeth, make sure it isn't dead before she feeds off it and she likes to pray to the Moon Goddess so its soul may find her before she feeds," I ordered.

"Ava!" Elizabeth squealed as she ran into my arms for a big embrace.

I caught her in my arms and spun her around.

"How long will you be gone?" She pouted.

I sighed.

"For a while longer Ellie, but I promise I'll come back. Don't I always come back?" I planted a kiss on her forehead and set her down on the ground.

I turned back to the pack house as I waved to Lucie and the rest of the pack before turning back to Eve.

"Ready Ava?" Eve asked.

I looked down at my attire and shrugged my shoulders. I was put into dirty ragged clothes to look like an escaped omega seeking refuge.

"Now remember Ava you're supposed to be weak, you can't show them who you truly are. No matter what happens, do not show them your strength, your wings, your weapons, NOTHING!" Eve shot at me.

"My anger will be kept at a minimum boss," I rolled my eyes.

"Good," She smiled.

We hugged each other as our wings wrapped around one another signifying a symbol of peace and balance.

We broke apart and took off our separate ways on separate missions, for the first time in a long time doing completely different missions.

I flew north as I tried concentrating hard to look into the mind of someone in the Blood moon pack.

Then I heard it.

'Stuck on patrol duty again on the full moon, no one would dare attack our pack even if they had the man power, Alpha Derek would kill them in an instant,'

Bingo.

I opened my eyes and followed the gold trail right before me as I continued following north. For 3 hours I was forced to listen to the patrol wolf's thoughts, some meaningless, some vulgar but most just annoying ramble. Soon enough the gold trail began to dive. I blinked twice and the trail disappeared from my sight, I dove down into the treetops and landed face first into mud.

Again, landings were never my strong suit.

I said a quick goodbye to my wings because I knew it was going to be a while before they were allowed to be free from my skin.

I heard a growl from a distance so I decided to follow it, that meant patrol must have been nearby and they sensed my presence.

"Hello?" I cried out, trying to sound as innocent as possible.

A wolf jumped from the bushes baring its teeth, signaling for me to not move. I stayed still and observed as the wolf walked behind a tree and shifted into a tall blonde man. Scars were littered over his torso and arms, possibly to show all the battles he participated in as a badge of honor.

Or maybe I knew that because he said it in his head.

"Who are you and why are you so close to our borders?" He growled.

I cleared my throat and put on my best actress skills.

"Please help me, my previous pack was attacked so I escaped death, I'm just an omega by myself," I pleaded.

Damn I was good at this.

"What's your name?" He questioned.

"Ava,"

"Doesn't sound like a full name, sounds like a nickname,"

"But my name is Ava,"

"What is your whole name maggot?!" He roared in my face.

"Avangeline," I hissed, trying to hold back my anger as my skin began to crawl and my bones began to ache from the sound of it.

"Ava is much simpler," He smirked.

I buried my frustration deep down inside me to prevent anything from surfacing, anything that would expose me.

"Well you're too pretty to go to waste so I'll bring you back to the Alpha and let him decide what to do with you," He said as he grabbed me with his callused hands, scratching against my wrist.

We silently walked through the woods for about 15 minutes until a freaking mansion like building came into view.

It was bigger and grander than both Nick and Jason's pack houses combined. If he wasn't the killer everyone painted him to be I would honestly give him props for this pack house.

"Come on omega," The wolf yanked me forward into the house as I continued to admire the home.

It was even better inside.

The living area was huge, softest looking couches my eyes have ever laid on, huge flat screen television, all kinds of gaming consoles and reclining chairs. Across from that area was the kitchen which was just as gorgeous, stainless steel appliances, oak counters and marble counter tops.

Such a beautiful place.

I was dragged upstairs and we stopped immediately at the first door on the second floor. He timidly knocked on the door.

"Come in," a deep voice boomed.

We entered the room and I immediately recognized it as a office. The moment we entered the room I was hit in the face with the greatest smell that I couldn't quite describe. It soothed my mind and eased my nerves making me weak to my knees.

That meant....it was happening again.

I looked around the office and noticed a tall dark oakwood desk in front of us with a man sitting behind it. There were bookshelves covering all inches of the walls with books of all kinds surrounding us.

Seated behind the desk was a man looking down at what seemed to be paperwork in front of him, his dark brown hair messy and slightly falling in his face. He had very strong and distinct facial features like a sharp and prominent nose. He had a strong jaw with light stubble around it and his upper lip.

How desperately did I want him to look up and stare into my eyes so I could see the type of mate the Moon Goddess has cursed me with this time.

"Alpha I caught this maggot near our territory and she claims she's a rogue from a destroyed pack nearby," The wolf explained.

"Kill her, I don't allow rogues in my territory," He said coldly, not even bothering to look up at me.

"Yes my Alpha,"

"Wait!" I shouted out.

At the sound and sheer loudness of my voice he finally looked up at me. His grey eyes met my brown eyes and it felt as though I was being pulled into them. I felt my heart slowly mending itself from my previous rejection and it felt as though nothing else mattered in this room except for him. I knew I felt the pull between us but I couldn't tell if he felt it as well.

I was feeling complete and I craved it more, I wanted to reach out and touch him so badly I nearly forgot what my initial goal was here.

"How dare you speak to the Alpha like that," The wolf hissed but Alpha Derek held his hand up to stop him.

"Roman leave," He finally said as he stood up from his seat.

"But Alpha-" He started to say but Alpha Derek shot him a deadly stare causing him to instantly shut up and bow his head.

"Don't make me repeat myself," Was all he said before the wolf named Roman quickly scurried out of the room leaving the two of us alone.

"A rogue from the nearby destroyed pack? Do tell me what pack," He chuckled as he walked up to me and stood right in front of me, looking down.

"I...well um..." I didn't think that far ahead when coming up with a cover for this mission, it would have been easier if I were just in charge of killing him but that wasn't my goal.

"Can't think one can you?" He said as he placed his hands behind his back and lowered his head to sniff my scent.

"A human? A hybrid perhaps because you don't smell like a typical wolf to me but you do have a certain scent to you," He said as he continued to examine me.

It was like he made me forget everything in my mind, I couldn't speak around him, all I could focus on was that divine scent emulating of his figure and clouding my mind but I couldn't get distracted, not even for a second.

I slightly stepped away as I looked down at the ground and shuffled my feet.

"My name is Ava of the Dark Mountain pack, I am an omega and my Alpha Jason was recently killed so I took that as an opportunity to escape," I stuttered out.

"Ava," He whispered out as he continued to circle around me, almost causing me to go weak to my knees.

My name flowing out of his mouth was like a symphony to my ears that I constantly wanted to hear on repeat.

"I haven't heard anything of Jason being killed but either way that benefits me but you....being an omega and being my mate is definitely peculiar," He said as he stepped in front of me once more and reached for my chin to tilt it upwards so that I was looking at him.

"You're different, I sense a fire in you," He said with a smile on his face.

There was an eternal flame in my body that was far from dying out, a flame to show who I was and what I was capable of.

"I don't understand what you're saying, my mother was a human and my father was a wolf. I've spent most of my life being a servant in the Dark Mountain pack," I said with a slight shake in my voice.

He spent several minutes staring into my eyes before finally boarding his grin and slightly laughing.

"You're lying, it says it in your eyes. I can't kill you because you are my mate and that wouldn't be beneficial to me but I will find out who you are and why you're lying to me Ava and you won't like it," He smiled before grabbing my hand and leading my out of his office and up many flights of stairs throughout the building until we reached the very top.

He opened the door to a room that seemed to be an attic, it was small and cramped only big enough to fit one person with a mattress inside of it on the floor and a window facing all of the outside.

"Since you wish to pose as an omega then you shall be treated like an omega my Love," He smiled before pushing me into the room and closing the door behind me.

"This isn't how I should be treated but what choice do I have?" I muttered under my breath.

I sat down on the dirty mattress and tried to gather all that had happened once I entered this pack.

I frowned.

Was this the Moon Goddess's plan all along? To have me meet my second chance mate?

She just gave her highest ranking assassin the most dangerous, fiercest and brutalist Alpha in this region her second chance mate.

I wasn't sure what the outcome of this mission was supposed to be but I was sure in for a Hell of a journey.

Chapter 4.

I felt a soft hand continuously shake me back and forth as I groaned and rolled over, annoyed at the intruder for disrupting my slumber.

"Eve leave me the hell alone and let me sleep," I grumbled as I flipped over.

"I don't know who Eve is but you gotta get up, you're lucky the Alpha has sent me to come and fetch you instead of someone else," I heard a soft voice giggle that sounded nothing like anyone I knew.

My eyes shot wide open in surprise as a young woman appeared before me, smiling warmly at me.

I wasn't with Eve at all.

I wasn't at the white wolves pack, I was at the Dark Moon pack where last night I just discovered that Alpha Derek was my second chance mate, something I dreaded but also longed to see what it might lead to be.

The woman before me had to be in her late twenties, her hair was black and curly which was similar to mine. Her face seemed so smooth and blemish free against her brown complexion and her eyes were a dark chocolate brown, eyes I always favored because they reminded me of my own.

"The Alpha told me to take care fo you for some odd reason so I got you a change of clothes after I get you to wash yourself," She said as she got up from the dirty mattress I was laying on.

I nodded my head as I stood up to follow her out of this little attic I call my temporary home of stay. I followed her down the stairs until we reached another door, as she opened the door I noticed the walls were completely white except for every piece of furniture which seemed to be black from the bed frame, to the mirror frame.

"Black is such a powerful and underrated color, would you agree?" She asked as she looked back and smiled at me.

"Yes, I don't think people give the color black enough credit, they think it's darkness but I think it's light," I answered.

"So well spoken of you," She nodded her head as she led to me to the bathroom inside of the room.

I think I was going to like this girl.

She left me alone in the bathroom with a warm bath already ran for me and ready to go. I stripped myself from the filthy rags I was in and stepped inside the bath, moaning out in relief as the warm water touched my skin.

As I stripped my skin of all the dirt and grime from the night before, I stepped out of the bathroom freshly clothed and noticed the woman lost in thought as she sat on her bed.

"Your name? So what is it?" I asked awkwardly as I scratched the back of my neck.

The only mortal contact I've had was with the white wolves but any other contact involved assassination so this was a new experience to me, speaking with a mortal as if we were equal.

She looked up at me and laughed as she shook her head.

"The Alpha was right, you seem different, my name is Natasha. What may I call you besides omega?" She asked as she stood up.

"Ava is what I prefer," I shrugged my shoulders.

"Alright than Ava, I have to take you down to my mate which is the Beta so he can show you what your task are while the Alpha is busy," Natasha said with a hint of sadness in her tone.

I nodded my headed an followed her out of the room , wondering what was in store for me that caused her to feel such sadness for me.

*

*

*

'Is that all you got?' I thought in my head as I received another blow to the stomach as I felt a huge bruise form and then quickly heal just as fast.

The wolf named Roman hitting me still didn't look satisfied at my reactions. His hits were nothing but mosquito bites to me but I tried my best to pretend like I was hurt but my fast rejuvenation wasn't helping the situation.

"Every time I fucking hit you, they just heal," He muttered to himself as he punched me square in the jaw.

My hands were tied behind my back against a tree as I was forbidden to move, it was such a cruel task I wondered how a normal omega would be able to put up with something like this but it was alright for me because training with Eve was so much more worse and unbearable.

I turned my head as I spit blood out of my mouth and smirked at him, mocking him.

Just as he cocked his fist back we both heard a growl and then that same smell from before that found its way through my skin as it managed to wrap around my bones and put them in a state of tranquility. I knew he was behind me based off the direction of the growl and his smell.

But I wanted him much closer.

"That's enough Roman, leave now," He ordered in his authoritative Alpha tone as he stepped forward so that he was now in clear view.

Roman bowed and before he briskly walked away he shot me a nasty glare before disappearing from our view.

Alex Derek stepped in front of me as he began examining my body, an occasional hum escaping his lips sending butterflies through my stomach.

"For a supposed omega you heal even faster than a normal pure blood," He stated as his hand gently grazed my jaw sending a slight shock between the both of us.

"My parents always said I was different from everyone else," I tried to lie innocently.

He looked me deep into my eyes with a bored expression plastered on his face, it was like be was boring deep into my soul, something I wasn't familiar with when it came to mortals.

"Still going along with this story of yours? Fine then, if you wish to be perceived as weak then I'll play along with your little game until you have no choice but to snap but I will warn you my dear," He leaned in closer to my face as he reached behind me and untied the rope restricting me like it was nothing.

"I won't be playing fair even for my mate," He whispered into my face as he smirked maliciously.

His words seemed playful but his tone made it appear as a threat and I wasn't sure how to perceive this but for some reason it excited me and I wanted more of it.

"Are you going to answer me or are you going to continue to stare at me like an idiot?" I snapped out of my daze to see him staring at me with a middle annoyed and mildly amused expression on his face.

"Excuse me?" I tried to ask innocently without sounding confused.

"Do you know how to cook is what I asked?" He asked now slightly impatiently.

"Sort of," I answered as I looked down at the ground.

"Fine, go in there and help the other omegas cook Ava," He demanded in his deep voice with a slight twinkle in his eyes.

I quickly scurried out of his sight as the butterflies continued to flutter in my stomach making me nervous and excited confusing myself since I hadn't felt this strongly in years. Not even with Nicholas did I ever feel such strong emotions.

As I walked into the pack house and towards the kitchen I noticed a small red head girl running around in the kitchen in such a frantic state.

"Do you need some help? I asked as I walked into the kitchen.

She turned to me with wide green eyes, eyes that reminded me so much of Elizabeth and made me miss her for a moment but I knew she was in safe hands.

"Yes please! This is an enormous pack of hungry wolves and the Alpha has instructed me to serve everyone food as a treat, if we don't finish in time we will be punished," She said with a terrified expression on her face.

I nodded my head as I walked into the kitchen and immediately began helping her with anything else she needed as we both scurried around the kitchen. It left a nasty taste in the back of my throat, being the one that was bossed around and the one who had to serve these ungrateful mortals who treated omegas like they were scum. As soon as all the food was served and the kitchen was cleaned I excused myself from the scene and tried to make my way towards where temporary room as I thought about my mate.

I wasn't sure if this was necessarily a good or bad second chance mate but I wasn't sure of the intentions of the Moon Goddess herself either. Of all the Angels why was I the only one given a mate let alone two? How could it be possible for an immortal Angel like myself to be the mate of someone mortal like Alpha Derek?

He reminded me of myself in some ways, confident in himself, cocky you could say. Power radiated off of him and he refused to take bullshit from anyone less than him, maybe that was why he was treating me the way he was.

I smiled down at the floor just thinking about him as I bit my lip but soon I felt myself walk into something sturdy and hard. I prepared for myself to fall backwards but I soon felt a pair of arms wrap around me as they caught my fall and the smell around them soothed my senses.

I looked up to see Alpha Derek staring intensely at me as he held me in his arms, wrapped around my waist. I noticed an emotion flash on his eyes but quickly disappeared as I tried to register it and it was replaced with a growl. He removed his arms from my waist and instead grabbed for my wrist.

I couldn't ignore the sparks shooting up my arm like fireworks as he led me to his office and closed the door as he slammed me against the wall with his hands on either side of my head.

"Clumsy aren't you Love? Are you purposefully running into me to get a rise out of me?" He growled into my face as he bore into my soul.

I rolled my eyes as I tried to hold back my fits of giggles from his seriousness.

"Don't you dare roll your eyes at me, since you want to assume the role of an omega you need to act like an omega and obey me is that clear?" He growled in my face, still not believing the omega story.

Nervousness began to set in as I realized he was not believing the omega cover story, how was I supposed to complete the mission if the person I needed to believe me wouldn't believe me at all, I had never failed a mission, never in my eternal life and I didn't want to start now.

Derek's gaze never flickered away from mine as I felt a sudden urge to reach up and rake my fingers through his soft and slightly dampened hair. His scent wrapping around him seemed to fill my nose and cloud my mind causing it to go fuzzy inside as a strong pull between the two of us could be felt in this instant.

I had never heard of a mate pull being this strong only on the second day but yet here we were in this predicament. I bit my bottom lip hard as I tried to concentrate on something but unfortunately that something else became his soft plump lips.

My breath hitched in the back of my throat as I looked up into his eyes and for a quick moment I thought I saw lust clouding his vision. My heart beat began to quicken as sweat slightly trickled down my forehead. Before I could react in any way Alpha Derek did something that shocked me.

He kissed me.

He crashed his lips onto mine and immediately butterflies began to erupt in my stomach. Sparks began to erupt wherever he touched me as his hands traveled down my waist holding me still against the wall and my knees began to grow weak against him.

I wanted nothing more than to stay like this forever. It was like him all over again...

It was like Liam all over again.

Derek quickly pulled away with a slight angered expression on his face as he looked off into space with a slight troubled look on his face.

"Shit, get out right now," He said quietly.

"What?" I asked confused and slightly heartbroken.

"You need to leave right now and don't speak of this to anyone," He said seriously as he grabbed my wrist and dragged me out of the office as he slammed the door shut behind me.

What was the cause of the urgency? Why was he treating me like this all of a sudden?

Confused and annoyed I decided I was tired of the mortal games and I just wanted to be left alone to my own thoughts. I quickly ran out of the pack house, slipping past those around me and made my way out towards the forest where I sat under a large shady tree with it's leaves slightly blowing in the wind.

'You are THE black winged assassin Angel, you eliminate those the Moon Goddess no longer deems worthy, you are one of the bridges between life and death itself for the mortals'

I shook my head as I mentally face palmed myself, I was not the one to be wrapped up in such tedious and dramatical circumstances even when it came to my mate.

First I had a mission to do.

I looked up at the sky and noticed the sun slowly setting over the horizon but I refused to go back into the pack house at this moment. I closed my eyes and concentrated hard as I tried to locate Eve's mind throughout the world.

After several difficult attempts I was able to find her.

'Ew it smells disgusting in here...these bastards better stop looking at me like that or I'll stick a knife down their throats...wait she's handing me a cup? Is this juice? Seems to thick to be juice...OH MY GODDESS IT SMELLS LIKE ASS!

It's blood, I wonder what it taste like...'

'I hate to break off your little internal thoughts but you're actually starting to worry me,'

'Well it took you long enough to contact me, I thought you forgot about me and started enjoying the pack life,'

'Oh Goddess no, these creatures are animals, if they knew who I truly was they would be cowering at my feet. I was used as a punching bag this morning!'

'You didn't show him anything did you?'

'No he hits like a bitch, you can throw way better punches better than these wolves,'

'It's physically impossible for a female dog to throw a punch anyway,' She answered back like a smart ass.

'Shut up idiot, how is the vampire life?'

'Look through my eyes and let me show you,'

Each of the Assassin Angels were given different unique powers from one another, mine was peering into the minds of others whether that be telekinesis, looking through their eyes and locate wherever they were in the world.

I peered through her eyes as our minds connected, allowing me all access to her thoughts and vision and I noticed was in a dark and slightly damp place due to the fact that the sun was now setting, it appeared that she was sitting on top of a bed with a ghastly pale figure next to her, sleeping soundly, the only light available in the room was candle light.

'Who's the ghost next to you?'

'He's the clan leader that I am supposed to eliminate, he wants to claim me as his wife because of my immense beauty,'

'Well if you weren't disguised I'm pretty sure he would pick the sun instead of your ugly face,'

Eve and I talked and made fun of each other for the remainder of our time. It made me homesick since we were on separate missions and away from each other's eyes. She was my home and it was never the same when she wasn't around. Besides I would have preferred the vampires instead of the wolves.

All of a sudden I heard a distant growl on my end and instantly cut the mind connection between my sister and I but didn't quite yet open my eyes. The same smell that seemed to follow me around wherever I went filled my nose as it became my oxygen, my life support as I felt a pull between that growl and I.

I turned away from the direction of the sound and opened my eyes to see a glowing golden path before me, leading into the direction of my home far away but I sadly couldn't take it quite yet. I blinked twice as my eyesight returned back to normal and I realized that darkness had fallen upon me.

I heard another growl but this time much closer and more demanding, I turned around to see Alpha Derek standing there in nothing but shorts and sneakers as if he just came from a nightly jog, sweat glistening from his skin as he looked at me with a disapproving look.

"Why are you out here by yourself when you're supposed to be in the pack house?" He asked with a slight agitated tone in his voice.

Was he worried about me?

"I've been here all day clearing my mind Alpha," I answered.

"Stand," He ordered with much authority in his voice, I tried to make it seem like it had much affect on me but truthfully it didn't.

You could have gotten-, I was worr-, you aren't to leave the pack house unless you have my permission. Is that clear omega?" He asked as as he stuttered his words, making it nearly impossible to understand what he was trying to say.

He turned his back to me again and began to walk away but I had a question boiling inside of me, one that for some reason I couldn't harbor inside of me anymore.

So what about us?" I blurted out.

He froze.

As he slowly turned back around to face me I noticed a look of bewilderment and surprise written all over his face.

He began to walk forward which caused me to walk backwards until I felt my back pressed up against a tree. I felt excitement and fear in the pit of my stomach as he stepped closer and closer towards me.

I held my arms out in front of me but he only grabbed them and slammed them up above my head.

I couldn't ignore the tingles that ignited as he gripped my wrist and held them above my head. I felt the bark of the tree stab into my back as he had me pressed against it. I bit my lip, not from excitement but from fear. He raised his lips up to my ear and growled.

"There is nothing between you and I. You don't deserve to become the Luna of my pack, you are weak." He hissed into my ear. I felt him smirk against my cheek confusing me.

"Is this what you are expecting me to say since you are an 'omega'? Until you speak about whom you truly are there is nothing between us," He said before turning away and walking in the opposite direction.

I watched as he walked out of the forest. I heard my heart shattering to pieces.

If only he knew my past.

What was I supposed to do?

Chapter 5.

A /N: (I do not answer disrespect, rudeness and inconsiderate messages.)

I felt a gentle hand shake me out of my slumber as I opened my eyes and was welcomed not by Natasha but by someone different. She was a young and beautiful woman with shoulder length blonde hair and vibrant green eyes that seemed to call out to you. Eve would disagree and say she seemed like any other mortal no different.

"Good morning!" She chirped happily in my ear.

I groaned as I sat up and looked around in my pitiful temporary room, remembering the details of last night's confrontation between Alpha Derek and I.

"Come on sleepy head you have to get up, Natasha sent me to come and get you so she could prepare for your task today. Derek insisted she be in charge of you bu I was curious to see what omega caught his attention," She smirked slightly as she closely observed me.

"Preparing me to do what?" I asked sleepily.

I came to my senses and just realized that she didn't address him as 'Alpha' or 'Alpha Derek', that must have meant she was a relative or close friend of his because the way he carried himself in this pack showed that he was a well respected leader.

"She's currently training with her mate and I've been told to inform you that you will be assisting them today...I must say you are very pretty to be an omega and it's a shame really," She said before turning around to walk out of the room leaving me alone.

"Bitch," I muttered under my breath as I climbed from my make shift bed to start my already brutal day.

As I finally gathered myself I walked out of the room and headed down to the very first floor where I noticed the beautiful blonde woman sitting at the island in the kitchen as she tapped her long finger nails against the marble counter as if becoming impatient with me.

"Took you long enough silly, my name is Taylor by the way," She said as she got up to shake my hand eagerly.

"Ava," I said curtly as I reluctantly shook her hand.

She led me outside towards the training center where I noticed a lot of the wolves from the pack sparring with each other and training as if it were a routine.

"Beta Daniel! Tasha!" Taylor called out as she waved over to Natasha and a tall dark skinned man beside her as we continued walking towards them.

Natasha outstretched her arms as Tasha quickly fell into them and giving her a tight embrace as if it had been a while since they had seen each other.

"Where have you been these past couple days? It's like I haven't seen you at all," Natasha asked curiously as they broke away from their embrace.

Taylor blushed.

"He wouldn't let me leave his room for the past few days and he wouldn't tell me why,"

Natasha turned to me and smiled as she politely nodded to me.

"Hi Ava, excited to train with us? I asked Alpha Derek if we could take you for the day so you wouldn't have to deal with being a punching bag," She said casually.

I shrugged my shoulders, not really caring where I was placed because it wasn't as if a mortal could do any serious damage to me.

"Oh by the way this is Beta Daniel, my mate," She said as she motioned to the man beside her.

He growled as he sent me a lot of intimidating expecting me to growl. I forced myself to bow in front of him as his growls didn't send intimidation through me but more so annoyance at the entitlement these mortals had.

Natasha grabbed my hand as she pulled me forward to the center of the training field. I noticed a tray of silver knives beside me, gleaming in the sun as the rays reflected from their surface.

"Ava are you fast?" Natasha asked.

Sure I was pretty fast, I could be faster than a bullet. I once killed five men in under twenty seconds, I once battled Eva in the sky breaking the sound barrier but of course I couldn't reveal this to them.

"I guess I'm pretty fast," I said shyly.

Who knew I could be such a great actress.

"We shall see," She chuckled.

She handed me a pair of thick protective gloves as she instructed me to put them on, this confused me at first but then I remembered that wolves couldn't touch pure silver as it burned their skin like the sun did to vampires and they all believed that I was one of them. I put the gloves on each of my hands and grabbed five knives in each hand. I watched as Daniel and Natasha got into attack position.

I slightly smirked to myself, this was going to be fun.

I there the first knife at Daniel and then two at Natasha so quickly their faces shown such a surprised reaction it was amusing. As they dodged out of the way I threw another directly at Daniel's face, he quickly ducked as he looked back at me with such an livid expression but wasn't this what they wanted?

I continued to throw knives as fast as I could but not too quickly to expose my strengths. As soon as they thought it was over and I was finally out of knives I quickly threw my last hidden one directly at Natasha when she least expected it.

She saw it coming from out the corner of her eye but not quick enough as it zoomed directly past her face leaving a long bleeding gash on the side of her face. She screamed out in pain as she clutched herself and fell to the ground bleeding and my blood ran cold within me. Beta Daniel turned to me with such an enraged look upon his face that when he walked over to me I already knew his intentions.

HIs motives were to hit me and to be more specific he was going to back hand me. I could have easily grabbed his hand to stop him from doing such a thing but that could easily blow my cover. I prepared for impact as he raised his hand with such swift movements and back handed me just as I predicted and I fell to the ground for the dramatic effect.

"Go to your room until I find a punishment for you omega," Daniel growled down at me.

I quickly nodded as I picked myself up from the ground and ran away from Natasha's screaming figure.

I finally let out a sigh of relief once I got to the very top floor and flopped onto the filthy mattress I called my bed, almost feeling sorry for what I had done to Natasha but again...this was what they asked for.

I stayed in my room throughout the entire day as no one had summoned for me and that was when I decided I would take matters into my own hand to find the Alpha so I could apologize on my behalf. I walked out of my room and headed to where I knew his office would be and as I headed there I noticed it was getting dark outside with the sun setting below the sky line.

I stopped at the first door on the second floor in the hallway as I opened it, not bothering to knock because I wasn't used to having to do such a thing but in that moment I instantly regretted it. As I peered inside I noticed Taylor only in her underwear as she straddled Derek behind his desk. He looked over at me, his once bored expression turned into a look of surprise as his eyes widened at the sight of me. The smell of arousal was thick in the air and it purely disgusted me, so this was who he'd rather give his attention to instead of me.

I could feel my heart dropping.

I slammed the door shut without another word as I quickly ran down the stairs and out of the house as I felt my wings pushing themselves against my skin, a pain I was all too familiar with. I wasn't sure why they were deciding to come out now, maybe because of the pure shock and emotional hurt that I was in. As I released them from their fleshy imprisonment I outstretched them as I soared up into the sky and stared at the moon with such hurt and betrayal in my face. I perched myself on a tree branch and sat down, looking around at the night sky. If only he knew who I truly was would he still entertain such a pitiful mortal?

If he knew his mate was one of the deadliest assassin Angels closet to the Moon Goddess would he still give her a second look? Was that look of surprise on his face because he didn't want to get caught?

My job was to kill and eliminate, so what was the Moon Goddess's end goal to give me an intel mission?

I swooped down from the tree that I was perched on and walked through the forest, back towards the pack house. As I exited the forest I heard hushed voices whispering madly, one of them almost excited.

I slid behind a tree and noticed to figures in the distance, as I looked over in their direction and tried to tap into one of their minds I immediately grew a splitting headache. I tried hard but was only able to piece together a few words.

'Angel.....killed....need....him.....war'

FUCK!!!

I felt blood dripping from my nose and I immediately knew one of them had to be Alpha Derek as Alphas and Lunas were the only ones in this world I had a difficult time tapping into their minds due to the protection of the Moon Goddess granted to them.

I looked at the other figure and tapped into his mind with ease, as I entered his mind and peered through his eyes he looked up at Alpha Derek and I noticed he was extremely excited.

"We were tricked, it was a trick to save the white wolf we captured," I immediately recognized his voice as the previous wolf from the pack I just recently attacked to save Lucie.

"The white wolf pack is heavily guarded and protected by the Mood Goddess herself that no one dares to go near them yet you thought you would be able to capture one without any repercussions? Sounds idiotic of both you and your now dead Alpha, perhaps he's still with them," Alpha Derek smirked.

I couldn't help it but his smirked seemed to melt my heart, the effects of the mate bond were starting and they were starting rapidly.

"No, it is a woman. The black winged Angel is a woman, I caught a glimpse of her as she took off with the white wolf, right after she killed my Alpha," The wolf said.

"A woman? Very intriguing, it doesn't matter if she is a woman I still need her. Find her, track her, I don't care how you do it I just need her to get rid of his monster before a war starts," Derek explained.

That was when I stopped.

I opened my eyes and watched as the gold figure walked away, I blinked twice so that my vision could return to normal and I could process the conversation that was before me.

What could he possibly want with me? Was this what I was supposed to gather intel on? What monster could he have possibly been talking about? So many unanswered questions that I need more information on, especially since I knew it all involved me. I flew back towards the dark pack house and noticed a opened window on the side. I dove in as I calculated the perfect time to retract my wings so that no damage was done and as I landed I noticed it was the third floor hallway. I quietly walked up the stairs towards my room and closed the door behind me.

I laid on the mattress and couldn't help but replay the conversation in my mind. He needed me and it seemed as though he needed me for something important but if only I could just get him to tell me for what.

All of a sudden I felt a burning sensation spread throughout my entire body as if someone were lighting me on fire. I ripped my shirt off and noticed bruises forming around my lower abdomen as if my body were trying to heal itself because they kept appearing and disappearing again and again. I knew what was happening and at that moment I felt betrayed.

A knife materialized into my hand as I plunged it into my stomach and hissed out in pain.

Let's see how much he'll enjoy this.

It still felt as though my body was on fire but now as if I had drank an entire container of pure lava. I gripped the knife steadily and began dragging it upward, essentially cutting open my stomach until blood began spilling out around me.

The heat stopped and my gash healed instantly as I whisked away the knife and flipped myself over letting out a sigh of relief.

No, I didn't do this to cause pain to myself, I did it to cause pain in my mate. You see once bonded you can feel each other's extreme pain and to ensure that infidelity didn't happen, the Moon Goddess placed a curse upon the wolves so that if your mate were to engage in sexual intercourse with someone who was not their mate, a burning and intense pain could be felt by the other.

I hope that ruined his night.

*

*

*

"Ava come on, wake up,"

I woke up screaming in pain, not a physical but n emotional pain from the nightmare I felt like I was stuck in for so long.

I looked up and noticed Natasha sitting on my bed with a concerned look on her face.

"What's wrong, what happened?" She asked as she hugged me.

"I went too far Natasha I'm sorry, I didn't mean to hurt you I was just trying to help you train," I said as I hugged her back.

She sighed.

"It's alright I'm not concerned with that anymore, now what's wrong, why were you screaming?"

"Nightmare," I muttered.

She looked at me for a moment and then turned away.

"Daniel wants you downstairs to discuss your punishment. I tried to talk him out of it but he wouldn't listen to me," She said as she stood up and turned her back to me.

I noticed the gash on her left cheek was no longer bleeding but it left an ugly scar that may never heal again.

I nodded as I got up to follow her downstairs where I was welcomed by the menacing smirking Beta.

"Ava, I hope you slept well you little omega, you'll be Roman's little assistant for today," He smirked.

I rolled my eyes.

Roman had an eye for torturing me so he could figure out what was my secret to healing so fast.

"Beta Daniel did you call for me?" Roman bowed as he walked in.

I wish I could say that Roman was an attractive one but he indeed wasn't.

"Yes, for the remainder of the day, Ava will be yours to do whatever your heart desires, think of her as your own personal assistant," Daniel smirked as he nodded towards me.

Roman looked over at me with a gleeful cheer in his eyes.

"Thank you Beta," He bowed once more before he walked towards me and grabbed my hand rather roughly, pulling me outside. We walked towards the training center and he threw me onto the ground.

"Get up omega, we're gonna have a little fun today," He smirked down at me.

As I tried to help myself up I immediately got a blow to the face causing me to fall back to the ground as I groaned. I didn't groan out in pain but more so in annoyance at how my patience was going to be tested today.

To his disappointment my face instantly healed as if he had never put in hands on me in the first place.

"Why do you heal so fast?" He growled as he gripped me by my hair and pulled me up, me squirming in his hands. He threw me against a tree as my back slammed against the bark and grabbed a rope as he tied me still, stepping back to admire his work.

If only he knew this was and tree were like toothpicks under my fingertips.

Before I could react I felt a dull metal blade plunge deep into my arm causing me to hiss out in pain.

"Roman what are you doing?" I heard his voice growl over me.

I opened my eyes and looked up to see a very furious Alpha Derek staring over at Roman with such annoyance in his eyes.

Roman bowed before answering him.

"Beta Daniel has given me this omega for the day as a servant,"

"So torture her?" Derek questioned.

"I just wanted to know why she healed so fast,"

Derek turned to me as he pulled the knife out of my arm only to slam it into my thigh and watch as my arm instantly healed. I looked him deep in his eyes, making sure he knew that this caused me no pain. He pulled the knife out once more and like magic it healed.

"What an impressive little trick you have there," He smirked at me as he leaned forward so only I could hear him.

"You should see what else I have up my sleeve, wanna see me pull a rabbit from my hat?" I said curtly, breaking character for a moment, it was becoming impossible to play the role around him the more he taunted me.

"Your mouth is pretty sarcastic for someone of supposedly of such low ranking," He smirked as me, as if my reaction satisfied him.

"ALPHA DEREK! I've found something in the woods!" We both heard someone shouting from the other side of the training field.

"Roman quit torturing her so you can untie her and follow me," Derek ordered before walking away from us.

Roman angrily walked towards me as I smirked at him, watching as he untied me from the tree and quickly followed after his Alpha.

I quickly walked back towards the house to create distance between both Roman and I so I wouldn't have to see him for the rest of the day, I wouldn't want an accident to happen where I break character. I noticed Natasha and Taylor conversing on the couch and as I quietly tried to walk by to avoid interaction, Taylor turned to me with a big smile on her face.

"Ava! Come sit with us!" Taylor chirped.

I mentally face palmed myself as I reluctantly walked over and sat on the far end of the sofa, away from Taylor.

"Sorry you had to witness Derek and I yesterday, peculiar that you barged into his office anyway but I'm sure you'll understand once you find your mate," She grinned, almost as if she were bragging.

"Well I had a mate," I muttered to myself but she seemed to catch every word.

"Had a mate? What happened?"

"He rejected me because I was the weakest and lowest ranking An- I mean wolf," I said truthfully.

I truthfully never opened up about my past, especially about my past mate Liam except for Eve and Nicholas. He was a memory too painful to bring up in conversations.

She giggled.

"What do you mean was? You're still the weakest and lowest ranking wolf,"

I couldn't help but to imagine my knife in my mind, I couldn't help that it materialized into my hand behind my back and just as I thought I would lose control and slit her throat, Derek quickly came rushing in excitedly as he paced the living area back and forth, muttering things to himself.

"Baby what's wrong?" She asked as she stood up. She attempted to grab for his arm but he quickly swiped it away from her as he pulled something out of his pocket.

"She's near! She's been among us possibly watching I just have to get her to reveal herself!" He said excitedly.

I almost gasped as I noticed a large black velvety feather between his fingers as he twirled it around. Maybe that was why my wings were painfully sprouting out of my back, I was molting.

"The black winged Angel from all those urban legends but they can't be fake, this proves they are real!" He pulled out a white silvery feather that I immediately recognized as one of Eve's feathers.

He looked at me as he looked me up and down with curiosity in his eyes before beckoning me forward.

"Ava, my office, now," He said before walking away towards his destination.

Confusion clouded my mind and I turned to Taylor and noticed jealousy written all over her face.

Was I missing something? Had he known all along who I was?

I marched up towards his office and opened the door to reveal him sitting behind his desk with his arms crossed.

I closed the door and immediately he growled.

"What were you doing last night?" He growled.

He was talking about the intense pain he felt from me stabbing myself so he could feel what I felt and stop what he was doing. Once mates set eyes on each other as every passing day goes by the connection grows stronger and the more they feel each other's pain and emotions.

Right now Derek and I were in a stage where we felt each other's pain and infidelity.

"I have a better question, what were you doing last night? Didn't take you as someone who liked blondes," I didn't even try to keep up my facade of an innocent and helpless omega, I wouldn't stand around weak any longer while he fucked someone else in my presence.

"What happened to the sweet omega girl this past week?" He smirked as he spun around in his chair.

"Save the bullshit for your bitch Derek, if you think you're going to play me for a fucking fool then you're wrong," I crossed my hands over my chest as I stepped forward.

Soon enough his smirk disappeared from his face as he stood up and began to approach me with annoyance in his eyes.

"I'll let it slide by that you did not use my respectable title but what I will not allow is for you to disrespect Taylor or disrespect me with your foul language," He approached me as he towered over me, looking down.

"Then maybe you and your bitch should how to respect the mate bond instead of fucking each other like whores," I hissed in his face.

Instantly his hand reached out and wrapped itself around my neck, pinning me against the wall as anger began to radiate off him.

"I won't ask you again, what were you doing last night?" He hissed through his teeth as he slightly shook me, now a grinning beginning to creep onto my face.

"Giving you karma...bitch," I grinned as he removed his hand from my neck only to trail it down to my stomach where he lifted up my shirt to examine for any scars.

"Roman was correct, you heal abnormally quickly for a wolf, let alone a half breed," He muttered to himself.

All of a sudden the office door flew open revealing a wide teary eyed Taylor looking between the both of us...the little distance there was between us.

"Poor doggy is heart broken," I whispered in his ear before walking away towards my room to leave the two alone. As I reached the very top and walked into my room I closed my eyes and focused hard enough as I entered Eve's mind.

'If he touches my sister again I swear to Goddess I will tear apart all of his limbs and-'

'Seems as though I may be interrupting something?'

'Ava! How could you be so cool and composed while these monsters hurt you?!'

'Why are you watching me?'

'How did you know?'

'You're molting and they found one of your feathers'

'Shit, well that means you are too and you can't keep your wings in while you're molting,'

'Eve we have a problem,'

'You haven't contracted the information you need yet?'

'That's the thing, I think his secret weapon might be me and what's worse, he is my second chance mate,'

'Ava you need to find out what he wants with the you, do whatever it takes to find out the information but you no longer have time to stall and play pack!'

I opened my eyes and noticed a gold trail leading out of the window and as I looked out the window I noticed a golden figure crouching in the treetops. I blinked twice and saw Eve looking at me from the treetops.

She motioned for me to go.

I nodded and immediately headed out of the room as I made my way towards his office once more. I heard hushed voices behind the door before I felt a burst of heat spread throughout my neck as a stinging and burning sensation spread throughout my neck and shoulder and that's when I realized that meant Taylor was marking Derek as hers.

Flashback

I landed on the ground hard as my gray feathers quivered behind my back. They were so disappointing and small because I am the lowest rank of them all.

I landed in mud and watched as feet approached me. I looked up and saw a smirking Liam looking down at me with such a pitiful look.

"L-Liam how could you mate with her instead of me? I am your mate, your soul mate!" I cried out.

He bent down and pulled me up by my hair as I grimaced in pain.

"I am the Alpha and I can do whatever I want. You are the weakest of all angels Avangeline, how could I ever love someone as weak as you? I couldn't be with someone as weak and pitiful as you," He snarled.

Anger boiled inside of me, it was an anger beyond anger but it didn't feel as if it was mine. I felt a sword materializing into my hand and I watched as Liam turned red. I stood up and screamed as I pushed the sword through his chest as he fell to the ground.

I watched as the light slipped from his eyes causing him to become a empty vessel of what was once a man I tried to call my own. My heart was broken and now I was left with nothing but this pitiful wings and an eternal broken heart. If the Moon Goddess were to forsaken me like this over and over, how was I supposed to continue believing in my faith and believing in my Divine Being?

'I am sorry my child, I never meant for him to hurt you but now I have failed you, with due time you will understand why sacrifices had to be made,'

I heard the Moon Goddess speak into my mind, an angelic calling ringing in my ear canals.

I fell to the ground and clutched Liam's bloody chest. He was the only person I ever loved despite him not loving me back but now I killed him.

Why don't I just die with him.

End of Flashback

She was marking him as her own when she had no right to mark what was mine.

I saw red, nothing but red.

I felt my wings pushing out of my back painfully, wanting to be free from their prison of flesh and bone.

"Ava?" I heard a voice behind me.

I turned around to see Natasha looking at me with fear ridden in her eyes, confused at the transformation happening to my body.

"Ava why are your eyes red?" She asked quietly.

My wings pushed out of my back slowly and painfully, I ran down the steps as fast as I could, hearing Natasha calling for the Alpha himself.

My wings sprung out from my body gruesomely as I covered myself like a shield and I ran straight out of the door creating a huge hole.

I flapped my wings and took off into the night sky where there was a full moon shining above.

"WHY MUST YOU FIND EVERY REASON TO HURT ME!" I screamed at the moon.

"Ava how dare you scream at the Divine one like that! What is wrong with you?" Eva yelled as she flew next to me.

All I saw was red. I wanted to kill anything that stood in my way. I wanted to kill Alpha Derek for allowing that whore mortal to mark him. I looked and saw him standing outside looking up at us with wide surprised eyes. I darted down towards him.

I wanted his blood.

I was suddenly pushed off course and looked up to see Eva looking at me angrily.

"If you kill him then you will die because of the bond and I can't let that happen, I don't know what he's done but don't let it get to you," She screamed.

A silver bow appeared into my hand and I shot a flaming arrow at her. She dodged it as I sent another one flying towards her that missed her face by an inch.

"Avangeline please listen if you kill him then you're killing yourself. I don't know what he has done but please don't do this I need you," Eva pleaded.

I shot another arrow towards and it hit her in her left wing causing her to scream out in pain and be sent whizzing down to the earth in a ball of smoke.

I blinked three times as I had realized what I just done. I vanished the bow and arrows and dove down to catch Eva in my arms. As I captured her in my arms I flipped us over so that I got the impact from the ground and we landed hard causing my spinal cord break and instantly re heal. I noticed wolves running toward us and I quickly put up a protective dome around Eva and I so that no one could bother us in her time of healing.

I watched as her feathers slowly began to fall off. The burns on her back began to heal but she was knocked unconscious. Wolves surrounded the dome banging on it, trying to break through but there was no use, no mortal would ever be able to break through the protective dome of an Angel. I held her close to make sure she wouldn't get hurt even if she were practically immortal, I wanted her safe from harms way and the safest place was in my arms.

Tomorrow was going to be interesting.

Chapter 6

I woke up hissing in pain as I felt something sharp sink deep into my side. I opened my eyes and looked up to see Eve standing there looking down at my with her hands on her hips, glaring at me.

I looked down at myself and noticed a knife sticking out of me, lodged in pretty deep.

"What the h-" I was interrupted by a loud banging against the dome. I turned around to see Alpha Derek standing there with a frustrated expression on his face, it almost looked as if he felt betrayed.

The nerve of him.

With a quick flick of my wrist the protective dome vanished before us leaving no barrier between the two of us.

"Office...now," Was all he said before walking away towards the pack house.

I pulled the knife from my side as I angrily threw it at Eve, glaring at her. As I stood up I looked around me and noticed Eve's white silvery feathers littered all around the ground signifying her molting was done, she snapped her fingers and just like that they all turned to ash without a trace of her around. She outstretched her wings as she ruffled her brand new feathers before they slowly retreated into her back. I folded mine nicely behind so they wouldn't cause a scene as I walked around.

My molting process was not complete so I could not hide them.

We walked into the pack house and it felt as if everyone's eyes were all on us and I even noticed a few people gasped in awe. I couldn't blame them, stories of Angels were believed to be myths, made up or even children stories so seeing two in the flesh was almost unbelievable.

As we walked up to the second floor and entered Derek's office, there sat Taylor in front of his desk with Derek sitting behind it. I looked closer at his neck and noticed a very painful and difficult looking mark placed upon his neck as if it were forced onto him and that was when I remembered.

A knife materialized into my hand as Taylor stood up to try and leave but I pinned her against the wall swiftly with the blade pressed against her throat.

"AVA!" Both Derek and Eve shouted.

"I'm sorry! I thought you were an omega this entire time and I couldn't understand why Derek was so infatuated with you!" Taylor cried out as tears began to well in her eyes.

"That's not a reason for marking something that isn't yours!" I shouted at her, sinking the blade slightly deeper into her throat.

"I found out you two were mates so I felt threatened! You were an omega that didn't deserve the title of Luna and Derek has been there for me my entire life! I did it without thinking and I didn't even speak to him about it first please spare me!" She screamed out.

"Ava the blood of a single innocent mortal is not something you want on your hands," I felt Eve place a hand on my shoulder.

She was right, I couldn't stoop so low and kill a semi innocent wolf all for personal reasons, that's not why the Moon Goddess gifted me this power.

I slowly backed away from her as I whisked my knife away, still burning holes through her eyes with my own and watching her image crumble as she couldn't handle the heat of my gaze.

"Taylor leave, I'll deal with you later," Derek sighed as he sat back down in his seat.

She quickly scurried away, slamming the door behind her and leaving the three of us alone.

"I knew you weren't a fucking omega, you don't carry yourself like one, you don't smell like one and your acting is terrible. I just didn't think you'd be THE one that I've been looking for," He rubbed his face in his hands before staring me into my eyes.

"I was gifted a mission by my Divine that is why I assumed the role...I can't talk to you with that filthy bitch's mark on your neck taunting me," I spat in disgust, trying so hard to look away from it but I just couldn't no matter how hard I tried.

"After our little conversation in my office and Taylor found us I finally told her that you were my mate, she blew up and did what I least expected her to do, she jumped me as her wolf emerged and sank her canines into me. I nearly shifted and my wolf wanted to kill her but I used every ounce of resistance to not, that's when I was told you ran out of the pack house with wings sprouting from your back," Derek explained.

"This seems a bit personal, I'm going to leave for a bit and check the perimeter or go chase a bird or something," Eve said as she looked slightly awkward and backed away from us. The moment she stepped out Derek stood up and walked towards me.

"Weak isn't a good look for you, unless you actually are weak," He smirked at me as he continued to step forward.

There he was taunting me again, for some reason he knew how to dig under my skin and irritate me. I hated being called weak, I was constantly abused and told that I was weak all the time by Liam, the word was like a trigger to me and I couldn't help but react the way I did.

"Coming from a person that let that woman force herself onto him, seems pretty weak to me," I stepped forward and spat in his face.

"You're a piece of shit for bringing that up," He grinned madly.

"You're a piece of shit for calling me weak," I glared at him.

There was a tension between us that I couldn't help but feel as I felt drawn to him. The Moon Goddess always had a funny way of pulling mates closer and closer together, something I wasn't a fan of but even with I as an Angel, it was still difficult for me to fight the mate pull.

"How about showing just how strong you are oh great Black Winged Assassin," He taunted me as his fingers skimmed up the side of my body until he reached my clavicle where he gently caressed it before putting his hand back down.

I shouldn't be playing along with his games, I shouldn't be feeding into his tricks. He was trying to get a rile out of me and see how far he could push me but I couldn't feed into it.

But isn't that what made me mortal before?

Just because we were Angels doesn't mean we were perfect, and I for one loved being cocky and showing just how beneath me mortals were.

It was my turn to grin.

"Fine, five of your best warriors that you don't mind getting hurt. Then we'll talk business before personal matters," I said confidently.

"Fine. Training square, now," Was all he said.

I smirked in his face as I flipped my hair out of my face and turned to walk out of his office. I noticed Taylor standing there with a timid expression on her face that seemed to satisfy me.

"Oh Divine one I hope you can-" I put my hand up to silence her as I rolled my eyes.

"I don't want to hear another word from you, I'll deal with you later," I growled before I walked away to find Eve outside, admiring the outside of the pack house.

"This is a nice house, what ya think the value of this is?" She asked me.

I stared at her in bewilderment, confused as to why she decided to have such a 'normal' conversation with me. Neither of us knew the value of any material things, nothing was more valuable than what the Moon Goddess bestowed to us and unfortunately she bestowed onto me another mate.

"Why the fuck would I know something like that and why are you asking me that?" I asked her surprised.

She shrugged her shoulders.

"I dunno, seemed like a very mortal thing to ask, I don't really understand it either," She said before she grinned.

As we looked around we noticed wolves beginning to pile out in the middle of the training center forming a circle as a all buzzed around excitedly, some of them oblivious to recent events and some fully aware that something mythical was happening to the pack before their very eyes.

"What's happening, what are they all crowing around for?" Eve asked curiously.

"Probably to see me fight 5 of Alpha Derek's best warriors, might even let them blind fold me and tie one hand behind my back doesn't that sound frisky?" I wiggled my eyebrows up and down as Eve laughed and pushed me away.

But as her chuckling stop she soon turned to me with a serious expression plastered on her face, almost a look of concern.

"You don't need to do this, I feel like you're doing this to prove a point and no points need to be proven when you're an Angel of such high rank as yours," She lectured.

"I'm not doing this to prove a point, I'm doing it to be petty towards my mate," I said in all seriousness.

"Pettiness runs in in veins of even the fucking immortal, please don't do this," She rolled her eyes.

"Afraid I'm going to get hurt?" I smirked.

"Hell no, I'm scared you might end up killing a wolf and then I have to clean up your mess," She laughed as she pushed me away.

We walked out towards the crowd of wolves and as they began to notice us they quickly whispered amongst each other as they moved out of the way, clearing a path for us as we walked to the center of the crowd where I noticed Derek, Roman and four other large men waiting anxiously to see who their opponent was.

"lease tell me you are one of my opponents," I said as I stepped forward and cracked my knuckles as Derek smirked at me.

"You wouldn't be able to handle me, besides I'm sure you're very familiar with Roman right?" He gestured to the left of him as Roman looked full of glee as he slightly bounced up and down like a child in a candy store.

"Just because you are the so called blacked winged assassin doesn't mean I believe you so you know I won't hesitate to kick your ass," He smiled manically as he stepped forward.

I looked over at Derek with a bored expression as I noticed a twinkle in his eyes as he quickly winked at me and turned away.

"Eve, blindfold me and tie one of my hands behind my back," I said as I stood up straight.

'This bitch is underestimating me, I'll show her what real pain feels like,' Roman said in his mind as I looked into his thoughts.

I felt as Eve walked up from behind me as I felt something blanket over my face and darkness soon surrounded my vision as I felt the cold silver chains wrap around my body and arm.

I could hear others chanting different things all around me, all cheering for different people, only a couple cheering for me.

I focused my attention hard as I entered Roman's mind and looked through his eyes so I could view everything around me.

I noticed myself standing there, blind folded and chains as I was still covered in rags, wings neatly tucked behind me as feathers casually fell from them.

But I've seen worse days.

I outstretched my wings causing the circle around us to grow bigger from those moving back from my large wing span.

I felt my left ear twitch as I heard cracking and growling from a distance, my right ear twitched as I heard paws stomping into the ground.

There was a wolf running towards me from my left and by the count of 5 he would be close enough for me to immobilize him.

1...2...3...4...5

I quickly jumped up and landed hard on the wolf's back, not enough to break his spine and kill him but enough to push a disk out of place and paralyze him. I felt him collapse under me but as quickly as I put him out of commission I looked through Roman's eyes and noticed the guy on his right rush towards me while he assumed I was distracted. My left ear twitched again and I kicked the injured wolf fast towards the man to make him trip. Just as I thought he trippy dover the wolf as I swept his feet off the ground and he landed hard on the ground as I heard a cracking sound from his face. My right ear twitched as I heard growls and snapping coming towards me.

As it jumped at me I smacked it away with ease as it yelped and flew into the ground causing a few bystanders to collapse under its weight.

3 down, 2 more to go.

I looked back into Roman's eyes and watched as the man next to him tried to sneakily attack me, as he came from the side I broke the chains from my wrist as a bow and arrow materialized into my hand as I quickly launched one in his direction. His screams of pain filled my ears but I chose to ignore them as I whisked away my weapon and snapped my fingers causing a warmth to ignite in my fingers. I grinned as I played with the small fire in my hands before blowing on it causing excruciating screams to come from Roman.

I took off my blind fold to access the damage and shrugged my shoulders. 3 knocked out, an arrow in one's neck and the last with horrible third degree burns.

"You might wanna send these boys to a hospital," I said innocently before walking away from the crowd, leaving everyone in shock.

I heard Eve following behind me as she held her stomach from laughter.

"You should've seen the look on everyone's faces, they all looked so terrified," She said.

"It wasn't much of a competition anyway," I shrugged my shoulders.

"So you're saying it was easy?"

"Well obviously," I rolled my eyes.

I felt something plunge deep into my arm.

"IF YOU FUCKING STAB ME AGAIN I WILL KILL YOU EVANGELINE!" I yelled at the now running Eve.

I clapped my hands together and folded them together as I closed my eyes forming a giant protective dome around us so that it was just her and I in the middle of it, stopping her in her tracks.

She turned around to face me as she smirked.

"Well if you want to fight me th-"

I quickly shot an arrow in her stomach causing her to double over and scream out in pain.

She clapped her hands loudly causing fire to erupt from her finger tips and project towards me. I shielded myself with my wings and flapped them in front of me causing Eve to be thrown against the dome. I got out my bow once more and shot an arrow at her, passing straight through her cheek.

"FUCK!!!!" She screamed as she fell down.

I ran up to her to help her and laughed.

"Be glad it wasn't a silver arrow or I'd be cutting it out of your cheek," I chuckled.

I laid her down and grabbed the arrow as I snapped it in half.

"Pull the rest out yourself," I said while pulling the knife out of my arm.

I turned my back to her, taking down the dome around us and hearing her groan.

"Still felt the need to prove yourself with that little show?" Derek walked up to me smirking, that disgusting mark on his neck standing proud and bold making me sick whenever I saw it.

"Still feel the need to show off that disgusting mark of yours?" I spat at him.

Soon enough his smile faded, dropping to a serious expression.

"I think may be time to talk business then," He said.

"And what would we need to talk about first?" I said as I crossed my arms over my chest.

"What the mission was that was granted to you by the Moon Goddess?" He asked once again.

I paused for a moment, thinking if I should actually tell him or not. The Moon Goddess may have sent me on this mission to find my second chance mate, which was why she directed me not to kill him.

But why?

Surely she couldn't just be trying to play match maker, that's not who the Moon Goddess was, all of her decisions she decided for a reason, for a bigger picture but what was the bigger picture?

"You were looking for me, as a weapon before a war starts, what did you mean by that?" I asked him.

"He's destroying packs just as he once did but this time he's much stronger, he killed my family and he won't stop until he has the entire species in his hands and more," Derek explained with slight anger in his eyes.

"He sounds like another power hungry Alpha that needs to be killed, the Moon Goddess never gave me an order to do so," I shrugged my shoulders.

Derek looked at me for a moment before turning away from me as he looked up at the sky.

"He mentioned you once now that I remember it, saying how he had a mate once that he despised and in the end she betrayed him," He said.

I felt a tear slide down my face as my mouth was left ajar and there was a painful ache in my heart as I continued to look at his back to me.

"No it's not true, it can't be true," I shook my head as I whispered.

He turned back around to me with a disappointed look on his face.

"I don't know what you did to Liam but he's pissed,"

Chapter 7.

The moment I heard that name escape his lips I took off into the sky, stunned at what I had just heard. It couldn't be and I can't believe it, I watched as the life slipped from his eyes as I plunged that sword into his chest. I sat there for hours as I clutched onto his lifeless figure wondering what I had done to deserve such a cruel fate.

I felt something slam hard into me as I was knocked off course and sent flying into a boulder in the woods.

I groaned in pain as I rubbed my lower back in pain and looked up to see an angry Eve staring at me as she walked up to me.

"What the fuck do you think you're doing?" She said as she stood over me.

"Are you an idiot?!" I shouted as I stood up.

"No but you definitely are, you hear his name one time and suddenly you can't control yourself?" She asked angrily.

"You wouldn't understand, you don't know what I've gone through with him and to know that he's alive after piercing his heart with my blade... it's hard to believe," I said as I shook my head.

She attempted to smack me with her wing but I grabbed it just before she hit me and spun her around until she smacked right into a nearby tree.

She stood up from the ground and groaned as she rubbed her stomach in pain.

"That's no longer an excuse anymore, you are no longer the grey winged weak Angel that you were when you were with him, you have so much power, so much confidence and just that much closer to the Moon Goddess, plus you have another second chance mate who just so happens to be hot," She wiggled her eyebrows at me as she grinned causing me to roll my eyes.

"He's not hot with another woman's mark on his neck, it's disgusting," I said revolted.

"Oh yeah that's true, well we can talk about that personal matter later, right now we need to go back to the pack and go further into detail this Liam situation. If it's true that he is alive that he is that much more dangerous if he managed to survive your celestial sword," She said as she motioned for us to walk back towards the pack.

I nodded my head as we headed back to the pack side by side as if we both weren't combat fighting each other like any other day.

"Ava are you alright?" Natasha asked as she ran up to us as we walked through the clearing of the pack.

"Why wouldn't I be?" I asked curiously.

"You seemed furious the other day when you ran out the house the other day and I-" I cut her off.

"Where is Derek? I need to speak business with him," I asked impatiently.

"In his office,"

Eve and I walked into the pack house and straight towards the second floor, I opened the door without knocking once more and as I opened the door I noticed him sitting behind his desk staring out of the window.

"Done being dramatic?" He smirked as he turned around in his seat to look at me.

"Cut the bullshit, what exactly do you need me more?" I asked as I crossed my arms over my chest.

"As I said before, you're a weapon to aid me before a war starts," He said calmly.

"Why do you need little old me for some half dead old Alpha anyway?" I rolled my eyes.

"That's the thing, he isn't some half dead old Alpha, I don't know what his deal is but he may be getting help from witches or demons or something, he has a power that's hard to describe and I don't understand it but it seems dark and beyond my strength," He explained as he sat forward and looked me deep in my eyes allowing me to be entranced into the windows of his soul, light dancing within his pupils as mixed emotions that I couldn't quite understand.

"This has to be a mistake, I plunged a celestial silver sword into his chest and held him close to me for hours while I cried over the only person I loved," I said sternly.

Silence over took the room as Derek and I intensely stared into each other's, tension growing between us as I noticed a flame of jealousy dancing in his eyes.

"Do you have a habit of forcing sharp things into your mate's hearts?" He asked curiously and tauntingly.

"No but I was pretty damn close to doing it to myself that other night just so you could feel the pain, by the way how did that feel? Stabbing myself in the stomach while you fucked the other one?" I asked innocently to toy with him.

"It was a weak moment I will admit that, I shouldn't have done that to you," He said calmly as he broke away from my gaze and sighed.

"I'll search for Liam, I'm not sure how long it will take because if he's still a live he will be a lot harder to track due to him having such high amounts of Alpha blood within him. Alpha's and Luna's are a bit more difficult to tap into," I explained trying to break the silence.

Suddenly a headache began to erupt throughout my skull as my vision began to turn white and I looked up at the ceiling as I heard a voice calling to me from afar.

'You must protect the white wolves and continue the duty I have granted to you'

Her oh so velvety yet frightening voice seemed to shake my mind as I felt a sense of urgency throughout my body as my bones shook and the message was implanted deep into my core so that there was no disobeying it.

The white around me began to fade as my headache began to clear and I looked around the room and noticed Eve's now fading glowing eyes as she looked at me in horror.

"The white wolves are under attack," She whispered even though she knew we both received the same message.

I grabbed her by the wrist and pulled her outside quickly as we stood in the middle of the centre square and I put a large protective dome around us.

"I can't fly while my wings are molting, light them up," I said as I turned my back to Eve and outstretched my wings as far as I could so she could get every feather.

I looked up and noticed Derek on the other side of the dome with slight concern in his eyes, not sure what were to happen next to me. I heard Eve clap her hands loudly as a rush of heat spread all throughout my body as I hissed in pain from the fire spreading all over my wings as old feathers turned to dust and new feathers arose to take their place.

I watched as ash fell around me and soon enough the heat stopped. I ruffled my new feathers as they glistened in the sun from their sheen.

Immediately I took down the dome and rocketed into the sky on my way to defend the white wolf pack.

Chapter 8.

'Elizabeth where is Nicholas?' I asked as I pushed it into her mind as I immediately located her and knew she was safe. I could practically feel her fear transferring into my own as I zoomed towards the pac.

'Ava there are wolves attacking us! Nicky went to go fight them off and I'm scared!' I heard her frightened little voice tell me.

'Elizabeth stay where you are, I'm coming!' I yelled into her mind.

I zoomed through the sky faster than any jet or plane nearly breaking the sound barrier itself as I was determined to make it to the pack so that no one gets hurt.

About 10 minutes later I was hovering above the pack, surveying the surroundings and accessing the situation as I watched rogues scattered everywhere with a sprinkle of the white wolves trying to defend themselves. It was only so much they could do since they had such small numbers, midnight wolves along with white wolves were the rarest of breeds, plucked out by the Moon Goddess herself and protected. My eyes lit up gold as I looked around everywhere selecting my targets. My bow materialized in my hand as the arrows lit on fire, I pulled back the flaming arrows and began showering the wolves with them, selectively choosing who became my next victim.

I watched as one single grey rogue pounced on a white wolf and clamped down hard on its neck. I whizzed down towards the pack and crash landed down creating a giant crater in the ground, blowing everyone and everything back around me.

I stood up and planted a giant protective force field around the entire pack, blocking out the rest of the intruders and leaving the dead and wounded inside with us as the remainder pawed at the outside of the dome. I heard a growling behind me and turned around to see one single rogue still on their feet, trapped inside with us as it bared its teeth at me in a threatening manner.

I materialized a silver dagger into my hand as I glared at the wolf, crouching down in attack position.

"Right now I would be more than happy to end your pitiful life so lunge at me if you dare," I hissed at the wolf before me.

It stamped its feet into the ground as it growled before charging right at me which I presumed it would. Just as its grey figure jumped into the air I threw the knife directly at it, stabbing straight into its heart and causing it to collapse right in front of me, lifeless.

The injured white wolf limped towards me whining and breathing heavily as it laid on the ground, bleeding out in pain.

"Lucie you always have a knack fir getting yourself into the worse danger," I growled at her as I shook my head.

As she laid down in front of me I applied deep pressure to her wound as I felt the slight heat from my eyes glowing gold and that same heat began to spread to my fingertips.

Moments later I released my hands from her and sure enough, her wounds were healed and no longer bleeding.

I looked up to see Nicholas, Alpha of the white wolves pack, running up to me with such speed as he finally reached me and engulfed me in a warm hug.

"Is this hug because you missed me or because I just saved your sister's life once again?" I giggled as my winged wrapped around our embrace, bringing us much closer.

"Why can't it be for both?" He said as we broke apart momentarily for him to gently caress the hair away from my face as he looked me deep into my eyes, his deep blue eyes pulling into his loving gaze cause a heat to rise to my face.

"You're so mushy sometimes," I laughed as I pushed him away from me abruptly, almost as if I had a sense of guilt for making a man feel this way for me other than my mate.

But he's the one with another woman's mark in his neck.

"So is your mission complete? Where is Eve? How long will this thing be up?" He pointed up towards the protective dome around the pack.

"One question at a time geez. The mission has took a turn for the complete worse, Eve is currently at the Dark Moon pack where my mission is and for the time being only Eve and I can enter and leave this shield while you guys are in danger," I sighed.

I bent down to Lucie as I stroked her fur, feeling the softness of it in between my fingers.

"Lucie I may have healed your physical wolf form but when your wolf takes damage than your person also takes damage and it will take some time before both souls are healed so you need to remain in your wolf form for the time being or you will be in extreme pain," I explained to Lucie.

She whined as she placed her wet nose in my hand.

"I know, it sucks," I chuckled.

I turned to Nicholas with a serious expression and looked him deep in his eyes.

"When the pack is finally safe I need you to come with me and meet Alpha Derek of the Dark Moon pack," I said seriously.

"No fucking way Avangeline," He growled at me.

I never understood why my body had such a strong reaction whenever someone said my full name but I just couldn't help it. Something about it made my bones ache, my flesh feel as though it was being ripped apart, my blood seemed to run cold, every nerve in my body screamed out in agony, my nails felt as if they were repeatedly being torn from my finger tips and my brain rattled within my head.

It was a pain that I wouldn't even wish on my worst enemy and a pain that intensified more and more with every time someone said my name.

I jumped up as I materialized a knife into my hand and pressed it up against his neck as I gripped him close, pressing his back against the protective dome, a growing intense heat in my face as my vision flickered in and out of red.

"Call me that again and I'll glide this knife across your throat," I glared at him with piercing red eyes and a murderous gaze.

There were gasps all around us as I looked around, there were red figures everywhere and I couldn't make out whom was who so I blinked thrice to clear my vision. All around me were the white wolves and Elizabeth staring at me with wide eyes. Someone who was known to protect them from harm now threatening their Alpha.

I turned around to see Nicholas standing behind me with his hands up in surrender.

I looked down at the ground as the knife in my hand disappeared and shame took over my body.

"I'm sorry Nicholas you know it hurts and I've been on edge because...its happened again," I said sadly.

"You've found a second chance mate?!" Nicholas asked shocked.

"Shut up!" I hissed at him to lower his tone.

He looked me straight in my eyes before grabbing my hands and pulling me close.

"Ava who is it?" He whispered to me.

A single tear slid down my face as I turned away from him.

"Alpha Derek,"

Before I knew it I was being pulled into a bone crushing hug.

But I didn't want or need his affection, I needed Derek's affection.

I felt Nicholas dragging me towards the pack house, ignoring any and all questions from the other pack members as we walked through the crowd.

"Take Elizabeth to Bethany now," He shouted out as we walked across the lawn and he continued to pull me through the pack house until we finally reached his now cleaned up office.

The moment he closed the door for privacy he pulled me into another bone crushing hug.

"Does he love you? You're so beautiful and powerful how could anyone not love you," He whispered into my ear causing a chill to go down my spine.

"I-I don't know honestly, it's not like he hates me but he has a personality I'm not quite used to, taunting, constantly teases me, cocky, always has that stupid smirk on his face and sometimes its hard to read him," I explained.

"So you and him are very much alike," Nicholas chuckled.

"He bares the mark of another woman, whether it was intentional or non intentional he is torn between the both of us now. He has history with her, I don't know what that history is but as long as that disgusting woman's mark continues to rest on his neck he will never truly belong to me," I cried out as I rested my head on his shoulder.

"What does any of this have anything to do with me meeting him? I'm the last person he should honestly meet," Nicholas chuckled, feeling his chest vibrate against mine.

"We need as much help as we can get to stop Liam,"

He let go of me and looked into my eyes as a flame of horror danced in his.

"What do you mean stop Liam? He's dead,"

Flashback

I fell to the ground clutching my face as he stood over me with such a fiery rage in his eyes.

"You're so fucking weak! Why am I paired up with such a pathetic person?! I am a fucking God who should have been paired with someone equal to my status!" He screamed as he grabbed me by my neck with all his strength and punched me square in the mouth. I looked up at him with fear in my eyes and a sadness in my heart.

It wasn't because I was in pain, even if I was the lowest ranking Angel I still healed rather quick but his words affected me so deeply it was like they were ingrained into my soul, every time he hit me it was as if he were sending me a message physically, telling me I was nothing to him and that I was beneath him.

Eventually I started to believe him.

"Liam please stop I can't take this anymore! Why can't you love me the way I love you!" I cried out in the corner as I scurried away from him.

"Alpa Liam," He growled at me.

I cried and cried in the corner as my sobs turned into heaves and hiccups, as much as I needed to leave him for my sanity I just couldn't bring myself to do it, he had a hold on me.

"Baby stop crying," I heard his voice suddenly soften as I heard his foot steps walk towards me.

I buried my head into my arms as I cried harder and shook my head.

"Avangeline this is the love you deserve, you receive this treatment because you are inferior to me, not because I love you any less, everything I do is because I love you," He whispered to me as he bent down to my level.

He grabbed my chin and raised my head up so that I was staring into his now softened eyes.

He gently pressed his lips against mine, kissing me ever so passionately, melting away any and all hatred and anger I felt for him in that moment. I hated that he had such an effect on me, how he could easily manipulate me and sway me with his words but I just couldn't get enough.

End of Flashback

"He's not dead, I haven't seen him myself and I'm not even sure how it's possible but when I do find out I have a feeling I'll need all the help I can get," I said as I walked towards the door.

"Ava I can't, with my pack just targeted they will need me even more, I can't just leave," Nicholas said sadly.

"Whatever," I said a s I slammed the door shut behind me.

I walked towards Bethany's room and cracked the door open where I noticed Elizabeth snuggled with her on her lap while Bethany read her a book.

"Romeo o Romeo, where for art thou Romeo?" Bethany said as she faked an accent.

Elizabeth giggled as she smiled up at her.

"They talk funny,"

Bethany was like a second mother to her even though she was only eighteen years old, she was the mate of James, the Beta of the white wolf pack. She was the first and only person to jump up and take care of Elizabeth whenever I couldn't take her on a mission, meanwhile everyone stayed cautious until they learned she wasn't a threat.

"Hello Bethany," I said as they both looked up.

Elizabeth jumped out of her lap and ran over to hug me as she jumped into my arms.

"Hi Ava, Ellie wouldn't stop talking about how much she missed you," Bethany grinned as her blue eyes twinkled.

"Guess what little one?" I asked as I looked down at Elizabeth.

"What?" She looked up at me.

"You're going to be staying with Eve and I during this mission," I smiled.

She squealed as she gripped me tighter.

"Yay can we go now then?" She squealed.

"Of course we can, let's go say goodbye to Nicholas," I said as I waved to Bethany.

We walked outside, hand in hand as I noticed Nicholas standing in front of the dome as he looked up at the sky.

"Nicholas are you alright?" I asked.

He placed his hand on the dome but continued to look up.

"Maybe I shouldn't have rejected her and I wouldn't be going through this heartbreak with you all over again," He whispered.

'Ava, Alpha Derek is having a fit that you aren't back yet, he wants you back NOW,'

What a confusing asshole.

I let go of Elizabeth momentarily as I wrapped my arms around Nicholas as I pulled him towards me.

"We'll talk about this when I get back," I said to him in a serious tone.

I always knew Nicholas's feelings never died for me when we decided to break things off but the thought of him rejecting someone all so he wouldn't have to let go of me is insane.

He looked at me, love struck, it almost hurt to see that look in his eyes. If only things could go the way I wanted them to, Nicholas would be my mate and I wouldn't have to deal with an arrogant fool but the Moon Goddess had her own plans.

"I love you so much," He whispered to me as he gently placed a kiss upon my lips.

"I love you too Nicky," I sighed as I let go of him and grabbed onto Elizabeth.

The moment I knew she was secure, I outstretched my wings and jetted off into the sky, flying right through the shield.

Chapter 9 (Explicit)

(Sorry, premature publish, I actually wasn't finished typing but now I am)

I landed as gently as I could onto the packs territory with Elizabeth in my hands. I made sure to cast a protective shield around her body so that the sun's ray's could not penetrate her skin and kill her.

Eve ran over to us as she noticed my giant black wings and smiled down at Elizabeth.

"How are they?" She asked.

"Right now they have a protective shield around the pack since we aren't able to give them our undivided attention whilst on this mission. No one was killed luckily but Lucie was injured," I reported.

I placed Elizabeth down from my back and kissed her forehead.

"Your mate is in a frenzy," Eve announced.

"The fuck does he need to be in a frenzy for? I wasn't even gone that long," I rolled my eyes.

"Mommy you have a mate! Can I meet him?" Elizabeth asked excitedly as she bounced up and down.

"Yes you can meet my mate and make sure you tell him to not be an asshole to me," I chuckled as I grabbed her hand and led her towards the pack house.

"Is he as amazing and wonderful as you said a mate should be?" She asked.

I frowned, not even being able to fake a smile for her because I wasn't sure about that question. I couldn't lie to her, I wasn't even sure if it would be considered lying because our relationship was a bit...questionable at the moment.

"Ava! Haven't spoken to you in a while, I hope you've been doing okay!" Natasha walked up to me nervously as she smiled.

"I've been fine now that I no longer half to pose as a weak omega mortal," I frowned.

Her mate came from behind her and wrapped his arms around her waist bringing her into an embrace as he looked up at me.

"My apologizes Ava the Black Winged Angel for treating you so cruelly," Beta Daniel growled.

"Like I give a fuck about your apology," I grumbled as I walked away from them both with Elizabeth and headed towards towards Derek's office.

As we reached the door I didn't bother to knock on the door so the moment I stepped inside that room I instantly regretted it.

There stood a half naked Derek over top of a fully naked Taylor. Taylor was lying on the desk as Derek leaned over her with her hands pinned above her head in his arms, he had a look of lust, anger and disgust on his face but none of that mattered to me.

I quickly backed away and wrapped my wings around Elizabeth to shield her innocent eyes.

"Mommy!" She squealed in surprise.

"Ava wait!" I heard Derek call out but I had already picked up Elizabeth and headed out of the pack house in top speed.

"He couldn't have been in that much of a frenzy if he had time to pin another woman down.

I was beyond furious and I was close to seeing red.

"Mommy don't be upset," Elizabeth said as I collapsed to the ground the moment we got outside.

Eve ran over to collect Elizabeth and the moment she did I shot straight up into the air, not bothering to look back. I flew around in circles above the pack as I concentrated long and hard of the person I really wanted to see right now.

'Zachary where are you?"

I asked as I was finally able to enter his mind.

'The same place you left me years ago my beloved,'

'Cut the guilt trip, I need to be in your arms,'

'You know where to fine me my love,'

I stopped flying in circles the moment I opened my eyes as a golden trail appeared before me as I quickly followed after it.

Mortals have this interpretation in their minds that Angels were divine beings were perfect with no flaws when in fact we were the most flawed.

We all may not remember our past lives but we were all once mortals, living our lives flawed and imperfect. In legends I am viewed as godly, divine, perfect and powerful when in reality I was the most imperfect of the, all, relying on the word of the Divine to guide me correctly.

After the murder of my first mate Alpha Liam and my immediate ranking upgrade I became drunk with power. I felt untouchable as if I could have whatever I wanted in the world, including any man I felt fit. Then many many years later was when I met Alpha Nicholas and fell in love.

Or so I thought I fell in love.

I was terrified of being tied down, scared that if I let another into my heart I would get the same treatment as I did before.

So I cheated.

I told him we couldn't be together because of my missions when it was in fact that I was still emotionally unstable and using both him and Zachary as a means of healing.

Hell, I was still using Zachary but he didn't mind it at all.

Zachary was a golden winged assassin Angel a rank just below Eve's, there were nights I would go out and seek Zachary's attention, no matter where he was in the world so he could please me but in my heart I knew I was doing something shitty to someone who didn't deserve it. Just when the guilt began to eat me up inside I broke up with Nicholas and told Zachary I couldn't see him again.

Until now.

I dove down into the tree tops and noticed a little cabin glowing bright gold, I blinked twice and floated down in front of the cabin where a warm fire was lit, warming the surrounding area.

"Ava," i heard a husky voice behind me.

I turned around to see a tall, tanned skin man with brown eyes and dark brown hair, hair on the shorter side and a smile so dazzling it could send many melting. HIs wings were outstretched behind him, giving off their beautiful golden glow.

"You're so beautiful, haven't changed at all since the last time I saw you," He whispered as he approached me.

I felt my face heat up as I looked down at the ground slightly embarrassed, he always had this effect on me.

"Tell me what's wrong, I can sense something wrong in your soul," He frowned as he grabbed my chin to gently raise up my head so that I was staring him straight into the eyes.

I felt a single tear slide down my face.

"Love is such a cruel thing that I wish was never granted to me, why is it that loves I want to love me never truly do?" I asked as I turned my head away to hide my tears from him.

He grabbed my chin once more as he looked me deep in my eyes.

"Well I love you and I have always loved you, is that not enough?" He asked me.

"No, the Moon Goddess has gifted me a second chance mate and I'm not even sure if he loves me, it's like torture to see him around with another woman when I'm the one he should be with," I cried.

"Ava I love you so much, I've always wanted us to be together it just made more sense. I hated whenever you would leave to go back to that white wolf and be with him instead but I was so happy when I found out you two were no longer together all for it to come crashing down when you told me you didn't want to see me anymore and now this is doing damage to you," He said sadly.

"What can I say, I'm terrible with men, I'm only good at murdering them," I chuckled.

"Well luckily you can't kill me," He smiled as he wrapped his arms and golden wings around me, pulling me into a warm embrace.

"I don't want to think about any of this anymore, all I want to think about is you and I right now," I admitted.

"Then use me all that you want tonight, I'll never leave your side," Zachary said.

From my last mate failures I may have gained extreme power and strength but what I have also gained was emotional instability, something I needed to work on in order to unlock my full potential and my full power.

Something I needed to work on before I faced Liam once more.

"Ava I want to make you feel good tonight? Will you allow me to do so?" He asked.

I nodded my head as I crashed my lips onto his.

I needed this release.

I felt my large blackings wrap around the both of us, pulling us closer together as we kissed ever so passionately. I felt his tongue lightly graze my bottom lip as if wanting access to my mouth which I easily granted to him, our tongues dancing together as we deepened the kiss, wrapping my arms around his neck to signal I wanted more from him.

I felt him firmly place his hands on my hips to keep me in place, exciting me with our closeness, our bodies pressing together as the warmth of the fire danced around us, such an intimacy I craved.

I felt his hands snake down into the backs of my pockets as he firmly gripped my ass from inside of them causing me to moan out in pleasure from his touch.

We broke apart, breathing heavily from our session as he stared lovingly into my eyes with lust clouded in his gaze.

"Let me pleasure you tonight Ava, let me show you just how much I've missed you," He asked.

Whenever he looked at me I could tell how much he admired me, how much he wanted to fight to be mine but for some reason I just couldn't return the affection. It would make more sense for Zachary and I to be together since we were both immortal until the Moon Goddess deemed our time but I just couldn't see myself with him.

But I didn't want to think about that tonight, I wanted to be distracted by the thoughts of love or mates, I wanted to be selfish tonight and think of myself.

I bit my lip as I nodded my head, allowing for my wings to retreat into my back and watching his face light up with pure joy as he did the same with his wings and crashed his lips back onto mine, hoisting me up by my legs. I wrapped my legs around his waist as he began walking forward towards the cabin and before I knew it I felt my back being slammed against the wall, rough play was always what he knew I enjoyed, after living so long you begin to enjoy the pain.

I felt his hands remove from my thighs as they inched their way up to my breast, teasing and pinching my now hardened nipples, he knew this was teasing me and I didn't like it one bit.

"Stop teasing me Zachary, what happened to pleasuring me?" I moaned into his ear.

"Nothing wrong with a little foreplay my love," He whispered into my ear as he threw me onto the bed and crawled on top of me, grinning from ear to ear.

He grasped at the hem of my shirt as he gently pulled it over my head leaving my breast in clear view as he ravaged them with his mouth, his warm lips clasping around my nipples causing my back to arch against the bed and a moan to escape my lips.

I roughly grabbed a fist full of his hair as I pulled him closer to me as I felt him smile against my skin. He pinched my hardened nipple between his fingers causing me to yelp out in surprise, he always loved to tease me.

He sat up as he grabbed the hem of his shirt and began pulling it over him exposing his toned figure as I smirked.

"Someone's been working out have they?" I questioned as I dragged my nails down the sides of his torso.

"Can't stay skinny doing the Goddess's work," He smirked as he trailed his fingers around my waist and then down my pants where he unzipped them and trailed his hands further down.

I moaned out loudly as I felt his fingers gently brush against my throbbing clit before reaching down to give me a gentle kiss and then sliding his fingers inside of me, beginning to pump in and out.

I gripped onto his arms leaving scratches as my breath became ragged and I reached down to unzip his pants, pulling out his hard member in my hands.

"Fuck Ava," He groaned as I began stroking him in my hands.

I felt something inside of me building up, just waiting to be released as I tried to hang onto the feeling for as long as possible, waiting to be released. My body began to fidget as my release came closer and closer.

Just as I thought I was going to come he removed his hands from my pants.

"What the fuck Zachary?" I shouted, sexually frustrated.

He smirked as he began taking my pants off.

"That's not how I want to make you cum," He said as he slid my pants down to my ankles, taking them off of my person.

He slowly positioned himself in front of my heated entrance and began sliding into me with ease.

"Zachary." I moaned out his name and clutched onto his back. He roughly grabbed my hands and pinned them above my head as he began pounding into me, nothing but the sounds of our moans echoing from the walls, spilling out into the forest around us.

"Fuck me harder." I moaned out as he groaned.

He began picking up speed, thrusting in harder and faster.

He grabbed my leg and placed it over his shoulders as he let go of my hands and grabbed onto my hips roughly.

I grabbed his arms as I felt a deep feeling building up once again inside of me.

"Fuck I'm gonna cum," I screamed out as I closed my eyes.

I felt a wave of euphoria spread throughout my body as I screamed out in pleasure and shook from the overwhelming sensation.

Zachary's body began to tremble as I heard him groan loudly and something warm shoot inside of me.

He just laid there trying to catch our breath as we laid there, him still inside of me still as hard as ever.

He looked me deep within my eyes with such love and admiration and I just couldn't reciprocate.

"I love you so much," He said as he caressed my cheek.

I smiled as I grabbed his hand and kissed the inside of his palm.

If only I could say the same thing to him.

He bent down towards my ear as I felt him gently smile.

"Did you think that was all for the night? I was never a one hit band Ava," He chuckled as I felt his hand roughly caress my hip.

Chapter 10.

Sometimes I wonder what my mortal life was like, did I live an easy life or was there nothing but truant and pain? Was I a perfectionist or was I constantly making mistakes? Was I close with Evangeline or did we have a terrible relationship? Sometimes it feels as though the Moon Goddess decided to give me another chance at having a purpose in this life, to find meaning and yet maybe I was making the same mistakes as I was before, maybe this is a constant circle I keeping going around and reaching the same outcome.

"Ava you're thinking hard, what are you thinking about?" Zachary asked next to me.

He got up from the bed after a moment of silence as he walked towards the bathroom while I sighed and turned onto my stomach, stuffing my face into the pillow.

I heard Zachary walk back towards me as the bed dipped in from his weight and he gently placed his hand on my back.

"Avangeline your mind is racing I can feel it, you can talk to me," I heard him say.

I didn't want to react the way I did but it was as if my body was no longer in my control, as if there was some deep rooted pain in my name that made my body wither in pain.

I flinched as my body convulsed in pain and a headache erupted in my head as anger and pain began to surge throughout my body, flashes of red began to stain my vision before I stuffed my face back into the pillow, wishing for the pain to stop.

"Zachary you know I hate when people say my whole name," I hissed at me.

I felt him grab me and quickly flip me over as he looked as me with full concern and fear in his eyes, something I was not quite familiar with.

He looked at me for quite a while, debating something in his mind, as if he were fighting with himself about something but I couldn't tell what.

"Ava I love you so much and I know you probably don't feel the same way but I just want you to know I've always respected your privacy regardless of my curiosity but what I am about to do is because I love you and want the best for you," He said in all seriousness as his eyes began to glow bright gold.

"Zachary don't you fucking-" Before I could finish and back away he grabbed my head and slammed me down onto the bed with him on top of me, his eyes glowing brighter and brighter.

As he held me down I felt a sharp pain shoot throughly mind as I closed my eyes and wished for all of the pain to disappear.

He was entering my mind without my permission.

Flashback

I flew as fast as I could but I just couldn't stay in the air for much longer, my feeble wings just couldn't allow it. As my small grey wings finally gave out I felt myself spiraling out of the sky, too tired and helpless to even attempt to save myself from the impact of the ground. It was a magical moment, just falling freely from the night sky, there was no noise in the sky, no one else around me, just the clouds and the moon herself. If I could stay like this forever I could.

I felt myself finally touch the ground as my bones broke from the impact and my heart began to shatter for the loss of my mate.

I killed Liam.

I felt myself coming in and out of consciousness as footsteps began to surround me.

"Oh my gosh she crash landed!"

"What's happening to her, she's healing abnormally faster than anyone else,"

"The Moon Goddess foretold me about this... we were twins when we were mortals,"

I woke up with sharp piercings pains in my back as I sat up screaming in agony as my wings painfully pushed themselves from my back.

"Everyone leave the room now!"" I heard someone yell around me.

I couldn't see anything around me because everything was gold , blinding me as the world glowed a new color I never experienced before.

"What's happening to her?"

"I think she's becoming a higher rank,"

I felt my flesh tearing around my back as my bones shifted and my wings were beginning to feel much heavier than normal. Different weapons and tools began appearing in my mind as I felt something cold and smooth appear in my hand I would launch it around the room but it just kept appearing every time I launched it.

There were grunts and groans of pain all around the room but there were voices inside my head speaking so clearly that obviously weren't my own voice.

'Highest ranking Angel'

'Who is she?'

'She's really my twin'

'How has she of all people been gifted with his rank?'

I was terrified of what was happening to me, was I truly ready to die?

You shall be the strongest of all my followers and everyone shall know it. Your black wings are a symbol of your strength and fearlessness and you shall lead over all of your kind. All mortals will fear you as they should when you are reborn.

My vision cleared as it returned to normal and I looked behind me to see giant black wings sprouting from my back, destroying the interior walls around me as the room was crumbling.

End of Flashback

Another Flashback

"Nicholas what will happen when you finally find your mate? Will I not matter to you anymore?" I screamed as I punched the wall next to me.

Argument after argument between us made me feel as though I couldn't trust anyone with my heart, like they would all end the same way as Liam did, with my heart broken and my sword through their chest.

"Ava please listen, I don't want to talk about this right now I have a pack to run, I love you and that's all that matters so why can't you just see that?" Nicholas said as he paced the bedroom.

"But you never show me!" I cried out.

He swiftly walked over to me and reached out causing me to flinch badly, the reaction couldn't be helped no matter what I did but instead of hitting me he gently placed both hands on either sides of my face as he looked me deep into my eyes and all I saw was love and sadness, something I just wasn't used to.

"I know you've been seeing someone else these past few weeks and I can't even bare to look at you because you're breaking my heart, I don't know who or what he is but do you love him?" He whispered as a single tear slid down his face.

I looked away, unable to look him in the eyes and bring him more pain than I already was, I didn't love him, I was scared to love or be loved and I wanted them both. I wanted to be selfish and have the attention from both, someone I was never given but I knew it wasn't right.

"Nicholas I don't know if I can do this anymore," I said, looking away.

"Ava no, if it's true I'm not mad at you I just want us to be together. Please don't leave me Ava I need you, I gave up my everything for you," Nicholas pleaded.

I didn't know what he meant by his everything but his pleas were sending me over the edge, on the brink of tears but I had to control myself.

"Nicholas I don't think we can be together anymore, I am an Angel and you are a wolf mortal and in the end I'll watch you die. We no longer have time for each other especially with my missions, I'll only hurt you more if I stay," I cried out, ignoring the question in hand. I couldn't admit to him that I was seeing someone else besides him and ultimately cheating on him.

He nodded his head as he looked me deep in my eyes.

"Please at least let me love you one more time before you go," He asked.

I nodded my head as I walked over to him and crashed my lips onto his.

End of Flashback

Last Flashback

He turned his back to me again and began to walk away but I had a question boiling inside of me, one that for some reason I couldn't harbor inside of me anymore.

So what about us?" I blurted out.

He froze.

As he slowly turned back around to face me I noticed a look of bewilderment and surprise written all over his face.

He began to walk forward which caused me to walk backwards until I felt my back pressed up against a tree. I felt excitement and fear in the pit of my stomach as he stepped closer and closer towards me.

I held my arms out in front of me but he only grabbed them and slammed them up above my head.

I couldn't ignore the tingles that ignited as he gripped my wrist and held them above my head. I felt the bark of the tree stab into my back as he had me pressed against it. I bit my lip, not from excitement but from fear. He raised his lips up to my ear and growled.

"There is nothing between you and I. You don't deserve to become the Luna of my pack, you are weak." He hissed into my ear. I felt him smirk against my cheek confusing me.

"Is this what you are expecting me to say since you are an 'omega'? Until you speak about whom you truly are there is nothing between us," He said before turning away and walking in the opposite direction.

I watched as he walked out of the forest. I heard my heart shattering to pieces.

If only he knew my past.

What was I supposed to do?

End of all Flashbacks

I screamed as I threw Zachary off of me sending him flying through the wall.

"Why the fuck would you put me through all of that again?!" I screamed as I rushed on all of my clothes.

As I zipped up my pants I watched as he slowly got up from the ground, groaning.

"Ava it's far worse than I imagined, there is a part of your memories that is blocked off from both you and others and if the memories you can remember are like that then the ones blocked off are surely to be worse, I just wanted to know the worse of your pain," He said as he rubbed the back of his neck.

A silver dagger formed in my hands as my vision turned gold, locking onto my target.

Zachary had a special ability which was very similar to mine. I was able to see the present through the eyes of others and read their others, he was able to see the past of others, things they themselves couldn't even remember.

Ava please don't do this," Zachary warned as he held his hands up in surrender.

Just then a hot searing pain began to shoot through my stomach and neck causing my vision to go blurry and my body weak.

But I was perfectly fine, so that could only mean...

"Derek is in trouble," I said as I blinked twice and ran out of the house before rocketing up into the sky without another word. I couldn't let another mate of mine die.

Chapter 11.

I whizzed through the sky, baring the pain of my mate as I made it my personal mission to protect him from whatever happened to be hurting him and as I began to approach the pack I noticed a pair of silvery white wings circling in the sky.

But they weren't Eve's wings.

As I approached the wings I noticed attached to them was a tall dark skin man with low cut black hair and very strong facial features so prominent.

He was the other white winged Assassin Angel Elijah whom I happened to run into occasionally.

He approached me with a concerned look on his face.

Eli what's wrong, why are you here?" I asked the moment we were close enough for contact.

"I was given a mission by the Moon Goddess to keep you under control, I fear something is about to happen," He said nervously.

Another surge of pain shot throughout my entire body as I flinched in the air.

"I can't discuss this right now, I need to see something done," I said before I whizzed down towards the pack house as I crashed down onto the ground, racing into the pack house.

I noticed Natasha sitting on the couch with another pack member as she looked over at me with slight concern.

"Where is Alpha Derek?" I asked without hesitation.

"The pack hospital, I could show you where it is," Natasha suggested.

I nodded my head and she immediately got up and led me throughout the territory until we reached a large red brick building. We walked through the double doors and was welcomed white as nurses and doctors rushed around. We walked down a hallway until we reached a door and as Natasha pushed it opened I was welcomed to a shirtless Alpha Derek.

Body was littered with painful scratches and bite marks, lower abdomen heavily bandaged, a giant deep bite mark on his neck.

I sighed in relief.

"So was that payback? Was all of this payback towards me?" He asked as he looked up with an annoyed expression.

"What the fuck are you talking about Derek?" I asked, instantly annoyed by his presence.

"You went off and fucked some other guy to get revenge and that I will allow because I deserve it, I just want you to hear my side of the story, what I don't understand is why you decided to bring a shadow walker onto my territory to attack me?!" He yelled as he stood up from the hospital bed and approached me.

I almost forgot all about Elizabeth, I was so emotional last night I just left her with Eve and assumed she was safe.

"I decided to bring her because she is my daughter and I didn't bring her to attack you," I rolled my eyes as I crossed my arms over my chest.

"She's not your daughter, how can you stand here and say a shadow walker is your daughter?" He growled as his eyes darkened.

I walked up to him as I jabbed a finger into his chest causing him to slightly wince and back away.

"I will say whatever she is, I have raised that young girl and taken care of her since she was a baby," I hissed.

'Elizabeth darling where are you?' I spoke into her mind.

Silence.

It was as if I couldn't feel her or even hear her thoughts.

'Elizabeth?'

I concentrated hard to try and look through her eyes, as I was finally able to connect through I noticed her eyes were drooping as if she were tired. She was looking down at the ground and I noticed there was blood everywhere.

'Mommy? It hurts,'

"Elizabeth what hurts?'

'It hurts really bad,'

I opened my eyes as I was welcomed by a golden trail leading towards the forest. As I quickly followed the trail I noticed a pair of white wings sticking out from behind a bush.

I quickly ran over to the pair of wings and held back tears as I stepped into the clearing to see Eve kneeling over a very bloody Elizabeth as she was lying on the ground, surrounded by her own metallic smelling blood. Her fangs were clearly visible and her mouth filled with a blood that didn't seem to be hers. It stood out more against her pale skin as her veins appeared more visible due to her slight transformation from feeding but she still had her same innocent face she always had. Her clothes were drenched as I noticed giant wolf like bites all over her body.

"Ava you said a mate was supposed to love and cherish you," Elizabeth whispered as she noticed a stepped forward in shock.

I bent down to her level.

"Yes I did say that didn't I," I frowned as I felt a tear slide down my cheek.

"He hurt you mommy and he made you run away so I attack him for you," She coughed as more blood began to leak from her wounds and her skin became almost translucent.

I pressed my hands onto her neck, desperately hoping that I could somehow heal her but I couldn't. Only those of white wolf descendent were able to be healed by us Angels.

"Elizabeth you didn't have to do that, I would have roughed him up myself when I came back," I smiled as more tears began to spill from my eyes.

"Will I be alright mommy? I feel weird," She said as she realized what was happening to herself. She grabbed for my hand as tears began to to escape from her bright green eyes as she looked at me with such genuine love.

This was a different kind of love, something I could never experience from any man in my life, a love that didn't require my body or my status. It was the love from a child, a child that wasn't even mine. Someone who looked at me and saw nothing but their entire world. A love that I would never be able to experience again.

I nodded my head.

"Yes Elizabeth I promise you'll be alright, the Moon Goddess will take care of you from now on as you both watch over me from the Gates above,"

"She's so pretty mommy, she looks like you almost," She smiled as she looked up, staring at the tree tops.

The Moon Goddess always took the form of what you needed to see the most and in this case Elizabeth needed to see me, Eve and I were the only ones she saw the most and grew up with in her short amount of time.

"I love you, I'm so sleepy," She whispered to me as her eye lids began to droop and her grip on my hand began to feel weaker and weaker. Before I knew it I felt my body shaking with sadness as her hand went limp and her breathing ceased.

"Please don't go, not right now," I cried out as I picked up her bloody corpse and began to walk through the clearing with Eve watching me closely behind. I fell onto my knees as I screamed out in pain, a scream that could be heard from miles away.

I looked up and noticed the sun trying to peek out from behind the clouds so I spread my wings and slowly began to fly up into the sky with her small delicate body still in my hands.

I flew past the clouds as the sun's rays began to spread all over my body and onto hers. I watched as her body began to disintegrate under the rays until I was left with nothing but ashes in my hands and a broken heart.

Was everyone I loved destined to die around me?

He killed her.

He killed her.

He killed her.

He had to have killed her.

My body began to shake out of anger as my vision slowly began to run red, the sky all around me turning a deep blood red as I let out a blood curdling scream signifying my anger and frustration.

I wanted his blood.

Chapter 12.

Eve's POV

She wasn't supposed to get attached. She was never supposed to get attached to the child and I told her this the very night she took the child away.

Flashback

I landed gently onto the ground in our campsite as I watched Ava stumble and nearly fall before regaining her balance and standing up straight.

I placed my hands on my hips and frowned at her.

"Explanation now," I demanded as I pointed to the child in her arms.

"It's a vampire child, she's about 2 years old but she didn't belong there. I don't know what they had planned for her but I had to get her out of there," She explained as she looked down at the child lovingly.

I pulled out a dagger as I advance dover to the sleeping child, wanting to end this once and for all but Ava quickly guarded both her and the child with her giant black wings.

"Stay the fuck away from her Evangeline," She snapped as she peeked through the feathers of her wings.

I backed away in annoyance as I whisked the dagger away and stared at her.

"If you keep this child Ava you will get attached and if something happens to her then you might lose control. Rule number 1, WE DON'T GET ATTACHED TO MORTALS," I scolded.

"Shut up I won't get attached, besides it a helpless child and vampire children grow quickly so in a matter of two months I will abandon her," She said as brushed the child's red hair away from her face.

"I'll call you Elizabeth," She smiled.

The child slowly opened her eyes as she stared up at her and smiled back.

"Fine, but I want nothing to do with this," I said coldly as I walked away.

End of Flashback

Now she's gotten so attached that she's going to lose control of herself and what was worse was that she was the rare black winged angel.

"Well hello Evangeline, I was hoping to never see you again," I heard a voice from behind me.

I turned around to see a tall woman with blonde slicked down hair down to her thighs, she had extremely red and cracked lips almost as if they were constantly bleeding and in pain as she had bright honey brown eyes that seemed to shine in the sun. She wore all black from head to toe with no shoes on her feet because never once did she allow for her feet to touch the ground, she always hovered.

This was Ariel, a golden winged Assassin Angel who also happened to be a Mother Nature Angel. Ariel was one of only few Angels who had more than one job, as a Mother Nature Angel she was in charge of tending to nature, animals and other mortals as well as stopping those who pose a threat to the very Nature and Earth that she loves, hence receiving two responsibilities as an Angel.

We both mildly hated each other but she only tolerated me because she adored Avangeline.

"I told you that Ava is never leaving me, so why are you here?" I rolled my eyes as I walked towards her.

"I'm not here for you. The Moon Goddess has called upon me for a mission here, she said a danger that needs to be controlled," She explained.

I brushed the dirt from my pants as I walked out of the forest with Ariel hovering behind me close by and there stood Elijah, another white winged assassin like me and Zachary, a golden winged assassin. They both looked at us with curiosity as we approached.

"What's going on here?" Zachary asked as he saw me approach.

"The last time we were all gathered together like this was the day Avangeline became THE black winged Assassin Angel," Elijah pointed out.

"Did the Divine one herself call for all of you here?" I asked them all.

They all nodded their heads.

A burning sensation erupted all throughout my head as my vision began to turn white and I looked dup into the sky.

She was speaking to me.

'A danger has entered this land that must be stopped before she hurts herself or anyone else, all will make sense in time, trust me,' Her Angelic voice filled my ears before I was pulled back down to reality and the white faded from my vision.

"Well what did she say?" Ariel asked impatiently as she tapped her foot in the air.

"Ava is losing control, I told her not to get attached," I said as I looked up at the sky once more.

"So what does that mean?" Zachary asked.

I gulped.

"We have to stop her so she doesn't kill herself or anyone involved,"

They all gasped.

"She is THE black winged assassin Angel, capable of powers we've never even dreamed of and we don't even know the true power she wields. How do you except the four of us to beat her?" Elijah exclaimed.

It wasn't like she could kill any of us anyway but then again who knew the power she kept inside of herself.

A blood curdling scream filled the skies as they reached my ears, a scream filled with pain and sadness. A sound so painful and heart wrenching I couldn't help but drop to the ground as I covered my ears. I opened my eyes and noticed everyone else had fell to the ground, wings quivering in pain behind their backs as they rolled onto the ground also covering their ears.

Finally silence filled the air.

"What the hell was that?" Ariel asked as she hovered back onto her feet.

"Avangeline," Zachary and I said simultaneously.

I glared into his direction as he quickly looked away. I knew all about Ava and his predicament, from the beginning he knew just how unstable she could be but yet he continued to toy with her heart like a game.

He didn't deserve her.

I looked up into the sky and noticed a figure in the sky looking up into the clouds.

"What's going on?!" I heard a shout behind me.

I turned around to see a very shocked Alpha Derek and his pet behind him trying desperately to cling onto him.

He looked around at all of us, our wings glistening in the sun light as he stood there with a shocked expression, one of many few wolves to be in the presence of this many Angels.

I rolled my eyes and pointed up into the sky.

He squinted as he looked up to see Ava in the sky.

"Is she alright?" He asked with concern in his voice.

I glared at him as I materialized a silver dagger into my hand.

"You killed one of the only few things that genuinely loved her, of course she isn't okay," I hissed at him.

He held his hands up in surrender as a look of curiosity crept up on his face.

"The vampire is dead? I didn't kill her, I never even touched her it was Taylor that attacked the child when she noticed her attacking me, I didn't know she killed her," Derek pointed at Taylor with an annoyed expression.

"Evangeline," I heard someone call out from behind me.

"Not no-" I started to say before I was flung forward by a sharp pain in my back.

"Fuck!" I fell forward cursing.

I turned around on the ground to see an angry red eyed Avangeline staring hard at Alpha Derek.

She wasn't aware that Derek was not the one that Elizabeth, if what he's saying is true then that meant Elizabeth realized that Derek made Ava upset so she attacked him for Ava, Taylor being extremely attached to Derek because of her mark and her attachment issues noticed him being attacked by a vampire so she shifted and ended up wounding Elizabeth badly.

Either way Derek nor Taylor can die, if Derek dies then Ava will perish with him because they are mates, if Taylor dies then Derek just might die because of the marking which will cause Ava to die.

Neither of them can die.

"Protect the Alpha at all cost, he cannot die," I hissed as I pulled the knife out of my back.

As she heard his she outstretched her wings and slowly pulled out her celestial silver sword as she had it in front of her in attack stance.

I looked around and noticed everyone else in attack stance, weapons ready.

"Wait," I said as I held my hands up.

"Ava you don't have to do this, let's talk through this and get the story straight," I said as I got up.

"You wanted nothing to do with her," she said coldly.

She was too far gone, anger consumed her and violence was the only thing on her mind.

"I told you not to get attached!" I snapped.

She was a child in need I couldn't leave her! Now he's killed her so now I have to kill him," She said as she advanced toward him.

Ariel quickly grabbed Ava's wing as she spun her around, smacking her into a tree.

We may have just started a war between the Angels.

Chapter 13.

Eva's POV

Avangeline got up and threw her sword towards Alpha Derek but I quickly charged in front of him and took the sword straight into the chest.

Elijah took out his celestial silver axes and Zachary took out his sac's as they both advanced towards her at the same time, Elijah attacked from the air as Zachary attacked from the ground but unfortunately for them Ava was ready.

Her silver bow appeared in her hand as she launched a bow at Elijah as it hit him straight in the stomach, quickly guarding herself with her wings as Zachary zoomed at her with lightening speed.

"Ava this isn't you!" He yelled.

He launched a sai at her but she quickly flipped into the air and clapped her hands as flames shot out of them. Zachary dodged the flames with ease but was quickly smacked in the face with a silver bow.

"She can't keep fighting like this I'm calling out the wolves," I heard a growl behind me.

I pulled the sword out of my chest and flinched.

"Don't do that, Ava has powers no one has ever seen. She could wipe out an entire army in an instant," I said as I stood up.

Knives appeared in my hands as I began launching them at Avangeline, trying desperately to get her to stop as she blocked my knives, fought Elijah, Zachary and Ariel all at the same time. She was a beautiful killing machine determined to win.

I threw a knife directly at her face but she quickly pushed everyone away with her wings, grabbed thee knife in mid air, spun around and threw it at me in a matter of seconds.

How could she be able to move so fast and know every single move?

A light bulb went off in my head.

She could hear our thoughts.

As soon as I said that she quickly turned to me and charged at me until she grabbed me and threw me up into the air. I quickly steadied myself in the air as I looked down to notice she was being held back by tree roots. I noticed Ariel's eyes glowing a bright gold as I remembered that she was a Mother Nature Angel, she could control the nature around her.

"Eve are you alright?" Zachary asked as he flew up towards me.

"I'm fine I'm just dizzy," I answered.

I watched in horror as Ava broke free of the roots and quickly grabbed Ariel, she grabbed her by the wings as she grabbed her now flaming sword and chopped off Ariel's beautiful golden wings.

It all happened so fast.

Zachary quickly grabbed Ava as his eyes began to glow gold, slowly her eyes began to droop as she slowly fell to the ground.

I flew down to the ground and landed gently as I walked over to the now crying Ariel.

"She cut them off, she cut them off," Ariel kept repeating as she rocked back and forth, stunned at the after math.

I was in shock, I didn't know it was possible for an Angels wings to be chopped off.

Her once beautiful golden wings were now in ashes.

Elijah picked up Ariel and Zachary picked up an unconscious Ava. I jogged towards him as I looked down at Ava in his arms.

"She's in a coma, I didn't want to enter her mind because I was afraid this would happen but she took it too far. I don't know when she will wake up or what will happen she she wakes," He explained.

Alpha Derek ran towards us with clear concern on his face as he growled at the sight of Ava in Zachary's arms.

"What happened?" He boomed loudly.

"She's in a coma I had to stop her before she did anything worst, I'm not sure what will happen to you," Zachary explained.

"Does that mean you need to be touching her?" Derek growled possessively as he grabbed a hold of Zachary's arm.

Big mistake.

Zachary's eyes immediately began to glow bright gold as he inhaled deeply before Derek's eyes also glowed for a moment before ehe ripped his hand away from Zachary and stared at him in astonishment.

Zachary looked at Derek with amusement as he chuckled.

"I'll never understand why mortals no longer show respect to those superior to them, just because you're an Alpha doesn't mean you're at the top of the food chain," Zachary said as he smirked at Derek.

"You're a fucking piece of shit," Derek growled as he began to shake with anger.

"I showed you what you needed to see now go run along doggy and do what you will with that information," Zachary mocked.

Alpha Derek huffed, obvious conflict in his eyes before he turned away and ran into the forest, away from everyone else.

I wonder what just happened.

"What just happened Zachary?" I asked.

"I showed him what he needed to see and he showed me what we needed to know, he's a white wolf descendant by the way," Zachary nodded as we both noticed a woman standing int eh doorway, beckoning for us to follow her.

"I can show you all to the pack hospital!" She said as she stood in the doorway.

Eli and Zachary began to follow her but I on the other hand decided to walk into the direction that Derek followed.

As I walked away from the clearing I closed my eyes and imagined Taylor's small figure in my mind to channel my shape shifting abilities and before I knew it I had become the blonde haired and vibrant green doll herself.

"Derek?" I called out in Taylor's voice.

I looked ahead and noticed Derek sitting by the edge of the lake with his face in his knees.

He looked up at me and examined me for a moment before he chuckled.

"So which Angel are you? I knew you beings were capable of extraordinary wonders but shapeshifting tops the cake," He said before he turned back to the lake, watching the calming waters.

"How did you know?" I asked as I began to shift back into my normal appearance.

"I have her disgusting mark on me, of course I would know," He said.

"So you think it's disgusting? Thought you two were pretty close," I said as I sat down next to him, looking out at the water and realizing how calming it was.

"She's not my mate, she marked me without my permission out of pure jealousy, we are only close because we were all each other ever had so of course we gained some sort of connection from it but when Ava came posed as an omega neither of us knew what to do. I sensed something more from her but I knew if my instincts were wrong then could I possibly let an omega be the Luna of my pack? Once I told Taylor she felt threatened, after learning Ava's true status now she's terrified and regretful," Derek explained.

"You wolves are so strange, so you don't hate her?" I questioned.

"I've never claimed to hate her, teasing her and annoying her is my specialty. Why does she mean so much to you?" He questioned me back.

"She was my sister in the mortal world, from what the I was given the privilege to see from our past life I've realized she's lived a hard life," I said calmly.

"Hard life?" He asked.

"Lost her wolf, lost her pack, lost her family including me, lost her mate, kidnapped and tortured, sold to prostitution, killed and fell in love with an abusive Alpha. You should cut her some slack," I listed.

"Interesting, is that why she fucks every man that gives her some kind of attention?" Derek asked annoyed.

"Is that what Zachary showed you? That bastard," I laughed as I stood up.

"Ava may be one of the most powerful beings on the the planet but that doesn't mean she's flawless," I said before walking away from him, heading towards the pack house.

As I walked through the pack house I noticed the same woman sitting in the living area as she looked up at me with wide eyes.

"Are you looking for the infirmary?" She asked the moment she saw me.

"I would assume so,"

"Come on," She said as she got up and led me outside to what I assumed was the hospital.

"My name is Natasha by the way," She said.

"Evangeline,"

"We walked into a room where there, laid Ariel still in shock and in tears and on the other bed was an unconscious Ava with Zachary sitting in front of her with either hands on her head and his eyes glowing bright.

"He's making sure she's well," Eli answered as he noticed my face.

"She's slipping," Zachary whispered as his eyes still glowed bright.

"What does that mean?" Natasha asked.

"She might not make it," I answered, pale faced.

Chapter 14.

Eva's POV

"Save her Zachary!" I shouted at him.

I watched as he flinched and his eyes flickered from red and back to their golden color for a split second. I felt a warm hand clutch my shoulder as I turned around to see Eli shaking his head at me.

"You know better than anyone to not mess with an Angel when they are in the middle of using their ability, it angers us," He explained.

" I've been with my sister for what feels like an eternity, you don't think I know that?" I rolled my eyes.

"I'm just saying the magic involving the mind is very complicated and if you keep disturbing him then-"

"My sister is in the fucking hospital in a coma! I don't give a damn about anything else except getting her back!" I screamed at Eli.

"SHUT UP!" We both turned around to see Zachary staring at us with red angry eyes.

He focused his attention back to Ava as he calmed down, his eyes returning back to their normal golden color.

I huffed and stormed out of the hospital, impatient and just wanting the return of my sister.

I walked toward the pack house as I walked straight towards the Alpha's office and sure enough I slammed the door open and was faced with Alpha Derek himself sitting on the other side of his desk, just staring out of the window.

"Come to harass me some more? This time you didn't shape shift as Taylor," He pointed out as he motioned for me to sit down.

"Mortals are interesting creatures and you're my sisters mate so of course I want to study you more closely," I shrugged my shoulders as I sat down.

"Shoot me then," He smirked as he leaned forward.

"Alpha Derek of the Blood Moon pack, known as one of the most deadliest Alphas in this region, merciless, cruel and a bit of an asshole," I said as I leaned back.

"Is that what they're calling me these days, funny," He chuckled as he stared out the window and placed his feet up on his desk.

"So you're trying to start a war against Alpha Liam? How is he even alive? Ava killed him many years ago?" I began to question him.

"I'm not trying to start a war I'm trying to prevent a war but he's powerful, he has abilities similar to yours but I can't really explain it," He said.

I looked at him for a second, wondering if I could trust him to take care of Ava, to not make the same mistake as one once did with Ava.

"Liam used to be Ava's mate long ago, even before she became the legendary black winged Assassin Angel, at that time she was a grey winged Angel. No real job, no real powers, they are there until the Moon Goddess decides whether they deserve a real Angel position or to die. He used to beat her, abuse her, use her, cheat on her and made her feel as though she deserved all of it until one day she couldn't take it anymore and she stuck a sword through his chest, I can't remember all of the details because these were all her words but he pretty much put her through Hell," I said, watching his face closely as I explained her situation.

Anger, sympathy, sincerity and regret were plastered clear on his face as he followed my words, a million thoughts running through his mind.

Silence took over the entire room the moment I finished talking, looking up at him I noticed his eyes now closed as he breathed heavily before opening his eyes and staring back at me.

"The past is the past, this gives me all the more reason to rip Liams head of his fucking neck," He smirked at me.

"You know you remind me a lot of Ava, cocky, confident, a smart ass but kind of amusing to be around. I guess I can see why the Moon Goddess decided to pair you two together but what I don't understand is your little lap dog," I nodded my head at the painful looking mark laid upon his neck.

He sighed.

"I will say being surprised and attacked by a small woman as small as Taylor is not my greatest achievement but I honestly didn't expect it from someone like her, my wolf tried to kill her when she sunk her canines into my neck from her pure jealousy. I don't blame her since we both sought refuge within each other when we were both in vulnerable positions," He shrugged his shoulders as he stood up.

"How are you going to fix this though?" I asked.

"Well it's simple, I have to find her ma-"

There was an agonizing scream that filled the air surrounding us, a scream filtered with pain and suffering, a scream I was all too familiar with.

Alpha Derek and I immediately rushed out of his office and ran straight towards the hospital where the screams originated from. As we burst through the doors we noticed Ava on the bed, golden eyed and withering in pain while Zachary was still clutching her head but his nose was bleeding and his skin was turning pale.

I grabbed Zachary to yank him off of Ava as Derek rushed over and began whispering sweet nothings into her ear as he stroked her hair, instantly getting her to calm down.

"She's reliving her memories from the time she became an Angel to now, some memories are too painful for her," Zachary flinched as he laid there to catch his breath and steady himself.

"Why were you doing that?" I asked, now pissed off.

"I didn't do it, I entered her mind to make sure she was safe but instead she's been blocking me out, I only managed to capture a glimpse of her memories," He explained as he stood up.

I looked over at Ava and noticed her eyes were now fully open but glowing their bright gold.

"Will she wake?" Derek asked.

"Not sure, her brain is scrambled and in overload, think of it as a computer, restarting and trying to collect as much memory as possible. She could possibly never wake or something worse, the mind is the most complicated thing on this planet," Zachary explained.

"Funny how you know so much about the mind," Derek frowned as he stood up and crossed his arms.

"Well one has to know about the mind if their power involves the mind, Studying and practice. Ava helped me with a lot of that," Zachary smirked.

I ignored the men as I walked over to Ariel who was lying on her stomach with the bones of what once was her wings sticking out of her back, burn scars surrounding them.

I gave her a look of pity and sympathy to which he rolled her eyes and huffed.

"Don't look at me like that, I'll beat your ass," Ariel said with clear disgust in her voice.

"Don't be mad at me, I'm not the one that cut your wings off," I mumbled under my breath.

"So did you purposely put the vision of you fucking my mate in my head earlier?" I heard Derek ask from the other side of the room.

Oh no.

"Maybe, maybe you needed to see that she deserves someone better than you," Zachary said as he stepped forward.

"What someone like you? Yeah for sure," Derek rolled his eyes as he said sarcastically.

"What's that supposed to mean?" Zachary asked as he stepped forward again.

"It means that if she fucking wanted you then she would have you already right? You've known each other for decades and you still believe you have a chance with her or that you have her wrapped around your little immortal finger? News flash, no matter how long you live you will never win the girl," Derek snarled.

In a flash Zachary grabbed Derek and swung him out of the hospital creating a giant hole in the wall.

"Zachary!" I screamed as I ran over to shove him.

"Mortals need to learn where their place is nowadays," Zachary said as his sac's appeared in his hands as he stepped through the hole in the wall and towards Derek.

"Fucking idiots, my money is on Zach," I heard Ariel shout in the back.

"Maybe you immortals need to learn that everything doesn't belong to you," Derek growled as his body began to shake.

"She belonged to me that night, the way she was screaming my name definitely made it feel like she belonged to me," Zachary smirked.

Derek roared as his body began to shift before us, obviously his wolf losing control as I noticed his midnight black wolf with a patch of white fur on his back.

"Zachary you can't do this! He has white wolf blood in him and he's Ava's mate!" I screamed at them.

But it was too late, Derek already lunged forward.

Chapter 15.

Eva's POV

Men and their fucking egos.

Derek lunged at Zachary in his wolf form but Zachary quickly dodged out of the way avoiding him all together.

Derek must have assumed what Zachary would do so as he landed he quickly shifted his stance and attacked Zachary from behind, clamping his teeth down on the back of Zachary's leg as he groaned in pain.

"You sneaky piece of shit," Zachary groaned as he attempted to shake him off. Just as Zachary raised his sat in the air to stab Derek in the back, once again there was another scream filling the air of the entire pack as we all dropped to the ground to cover our ears from the pain of the scream.

Derek's wolf whined as he let go and pawed at his own ears, trying to drown the sound out. Just as silence overcame I walked over to Zachary and back handed him army vision slightly flickered to red due to my anger and frustration.

"How about you stop fighting and go help my sister like you're supposed to be doing!" I screamed at him.

"Evangeline I can't do anything, whatever is happening has to happen on its own. I'm officially blocked out of her mind," Zachary insisted.

Angry, I walked back to the pack hospital as I burst through the room that was holding both Ava and Ariel. She had finally stopped screaming but I noticed blood dripping from her nose to which I grabbed tissues to wipe the blood away from her face as I sighed.

"Eva she's in pain, I don't know how much more she can take anymore," I heard Ariel say from across the room.

I turned around to see Ariel staring at me with such a pained expression, it wasn't like she was bed ridden she just wasn't used to walking without her wings, she wasn't use to the absent weight on her back that she once had.

"Do you think they'll grow back?" I asked, ignoring her statement about my sister.

Ava was strong, definitely strong enough to get through whatever she was going through.

"Eli says they are growing back, just extremely slowly. I've never heard of an Angel getting their wings cut off so I don't even know if I'll be the same rank anymore," She said sadly as she huffed, laying her head against the bed.

"Have hope in the Moon Goddess, she is our all Divine Creator," I smiled.

We were never to doubt our Divine Goddess and that everything she did was for a grand reason but what was the reason for all of this? Hasn't my sister been through enough pain and torture in her life?

"Ava please come back, I miss your stupid, bubbly and serious self," I whispered to her.

"He murdered her," I heard her murmur to herself.

I looked down at her.

Everything was still the same, eyes still glowing golden and she hadn't moved a muscle.

"What did she say?" I heard Zachary and Derek ask at the same time as they entered the room.

"I'm not sure," I shrugged my shoulders.

"He murdered her," She said again much louder.

"Why is she saying that?" Derek asked frantically as he stepped forward.

"Kill him, he killed her, he deserves death," She began muttering to herself.

Everyone in the room grew quiet.

She was able to get away with killing her mate a first time but I wasn't sure of the consequences if she were to do it again. It was highly possible that she could die.

I told her not to get attached.

"Zachary I don't care how much you hate him but you have to do something about that, we can't let her continue to think this," I pleaded.

He looked at me for a moment, contemplating something before he turned to me and nodded his head.

"There is something that I can do but it will be risky," He said.

"Just do it," I snapped.

He walked towards her as he placed either hands on both sides of her head as his eyes began to glow bright gold. His face grimaced in pain as he struggled for a bit, blood began to leak from his nose as his skin turned pale once more before he finally let go with a face of fear.

"I removed too much," He whispered.

"What are you talking about?" I questioned.

"Eve?" I looked down to see Ava staring up at me with a confused expression.

"Oh my gosh Ava are you okay? How are you feeling?" I said as I pulled her into a tight hug.

"I'm fine but something feels weird, where are we?" She questioned.

I pulled away as I looked down at her confused and then looked over at Zachary. He pulled me to the side as he looked over at me nervously.

"I went into her memories and decided to lock all memories she's ever had of Elizabeth, if she were to forget Elizabeth then she would forget all about the accident," Zachary explained.

"Okay so?" I questioned, it sounded like a great foolproof plan, how could it have gone wrong?

"The mind itself is a completely complex system that no one quite understands yet, not even me. Locking the door on certain memories is tricky and dangerous enough as it is because in the process another one could be locked or another could be forced open and in this case I also locked the memory of Ava and Derek ever being mates, Ava's mind is strong so once it starts to piece together that something is missing it might reek havoc on her," He thoroughly explained the situation.

I did the only logical thing I could think of in this situation.

I smacked his forehead.

"You thought me to do something!" He exclaimed as he rubbed his forehead.

Ava sat up from the bed as she stretched her arms and yawned as if waking from a long slumber.

She looked over and noticed Zachary as she slightly blushed and stared at him.

"What are you doing here?" She questioned him.

"Mission," He muttered.

She stood up from the bed as she noticed Ariel behind her laying on a bed.

"Hey doll good to see you're awake, are you okay?" Ariel asked as Ava approached her.

"Shouldn't I be asking you that?" Ava asked with a raised eyebrow.

"It's fine it was only a training accident, they will grow back eventually," Ariel shrugged.

Ava's eyes glowed bright gold as she placed her hands on the hollow bones, slowly the bones began to grow until sure enough Ariel's beautiful golden wings were finally restored.

Ariel quickly hopped up from the bed as she squealed and kissed Ava full on the mouth causing Derek to grunt in the background.

"Thank you so much I fucking love you!" She squealed as she smirked.

"You're such a lesbian," I rolled my eyes.

"I shall not be tamed by these mortal rules when it involves sexuality, I am a divine being," Ariel stuck her tongue out at me.

"Eli would you mind taking Ava outside for a moment while we try to figure things out?" I asked Eli who was in the corner, not engaging in our shenanigans.

He nodded his head as he took Ava's hand and led her outside.

"So who else should I be aware of that is in love with my mate?" Derek asked as he growled.

"You don't even know the half of it. She just has this charm to her that attracts people, not to mention she one of the most powerful beings on top of gorgeous but once you get to know her there is someone inside her that is quite beautiful," She explained dreamily.

"You act like such a fucking mortal," I rolled my eyes.

"I've been at this centuries longer than you, you might want to hang on to that mortal sense while you can still feel it," Ariel winked at me.

"Should we take her back to the white wolf pack and explain what happened to Nicholas?" Zachary asked.

"Why would Alpha Nicholas care?" Derek asked.

"Nicholas rejected his mate just to be with Ava," Zachary admitted.

The room fell silent.

"How do you know this?" I asked.

"He attempted to hunt me down and actually did well of a job but he was determined to kill me so I used my power to look into his memories and saw him rejecting his mate, I vowed to leave Ava alone after that," He admitted.

"Why are you telling us this now?" Ariel asked.

"I've recently seen his mate and I feel like it could help us with a little situation," Zachary shrugged his shoulders.

"So then who is his mate?" I questioned.

"Taylor Abrundy," Derek smirked.

"Your fucking lap dog?!" I laughed out loud.

Chapter 16.

Eva's POV

"Well it isn't wrong to call her your lap dog if she's always on your fucking lap," I smirked at Derek.

"There's no need for you to pick on her just because she's been with me before Ava even knew I existed. Ava is the one that stole away Nicholas," Derek said.

I looked at him with confusion.

"The night I turned 18 I was told that I was going to find my mate and that she would complete me, that never happened so I ran away from home in search of her because I thought if my parents couldn't show me the love that deserved then my mate definitely would. My parents instilled fear, and pain into my mind, told me that's what it took to become a great leader. Instead of finding my mate I found Taylor instead and she told me she had been rejected and we've been each others comfort ever since," Derek went into detail.

"Nicholas fell in love with Ava before he even had a chance to meet his true mate Taylor and he knew the consequences of being with someone before meeting your mate so when he finally met Taylor he refused to give up on Ava so he rejected her," Zachary implied.

It sounded like they both were implying that Ava was the cause of all of this.

"Don't make it seem like this is all my sister's fault because you fuckers mistakes," I growled.

"No one is saying that," Derek growled back.

"Look arguing is going to solve anything," Zachary stood in between the both of us.

"None of this fucking matters at the moment, I looked for the black winged Angel because I needed help stoping Liam, now all of you are here and we aren't anywhere closer to finding him and stopping him," Derek said angrily.

"Well this does currently matter because in order to get Liam-" I started but was interrupted by Ariel who put her hand up for silence.

"I was not told to capture Liam or kill Liam or whatever the fuck you want us to do to a motherfucker that might not even be alive, my mission was to contain a danger," Ariel crossed her arms as she hovered over the ground.

"LIAM IS THE DANGER!!! Your fucking Moon Goddess did not specify a danger to contain and right now Liam is the danger!" Derek yelled out angrily.

Zachary, Ariel and I all materialized weapons into our hands as we pointed them all at Derek as a warning.

"Don't you dare disrespect the Divine Goddess herself, she has done more for you wolves then you ever will imagine," Ariel snapped.

Derek held his hands up in surrender.

"Eva we have a problem," Eli said as he walked into the hospital with a worried expression plastered on his face.

"Where's Ava?" I questioned.

He motioned for us to follow him outside and as we all piled outside I noticed a giant dome in the middle of the territory and there sat Ava in the middle, cross legged and golden eyed.

"It won't allow for anyone to go in or come out, it's as if her subconscious did it herself," Eli said as he shook his head.

"This is my fault, I thought if I could just go in and close a certain door in her mind then everything would be fine but now there's a chain reaction and her mind is trying to open what i locked and it knows things could get violent," Zachary said frantically.

"Good to know you're aware that you're a fuck up," Derek muttered but Zachary caught every word.

"You're of white wolf descendant right? I could fucking destroy and heal you in an instant," Zachary scolded.

"Fighting isn't going to solve anything right now, we need to focus on Ava right now," Eli argued.

I can't remember a time when Ava was this unstable and we weren't able to control her. Hell the last time she was this close to being unstable was when we first found her and she got her official ranking.

Flashback

I watched as the girl began to calm down, weapons ceased, eyes no longer glowing and now her beautiful black wings were folded neatly behind her.

I growled.

Who was she and who did she think she was to come in here and show off her newest and highest ranking.

"Who the fuck are you?" I spat as I approached her in the hospital bed.

She looked up at me with fearful eyes, eyes that showed her innocence and her pain behind them.

"My name is Avangeline. I am or at least was a grey winged Angel," She spoke quietly.

Avangeline...Evangeline...they were basically the same name.

"What has the Moon Goddess told you about us being twin sisters?" I asked in disgust.

She couldn't believe this woman in front of me was supposed to be my twin sister and the new black winged assassin Angel, everything about her screamed weak and fragile as she sat there looking so innocent and small, eyes looking as if she were to cry at any moment.

I noticed her eyes glowing as she stared at me, after a few moments she blinked twice and looked up at me with tearful eyes.

"I'm sorry I don't meet your standards of a sister," She whispered to me.

Reading the minds of others was basically an impossible power to achieve, the only other Angel able to believe such power involving the mind was Zachary and even then his power wasn't comparable to this in front of me.

"How did you do that?" I asked her.

"What?"

"The mind thing, how did you do that?" I asked irritable.

"It just sort of happened," She whispered.

I grabbed her by her hair as I pulled her out of the hospital bed as she clawed at my grasp, screaming and kicking.

"Evangeline what are you doing?" Ariel yelled as she hovered in.

I walked past her, dragging this girl until we reached outside. Before I knew it I felt something pull on my legs and in a flash I was pulled to the ground. I watched as she got up from the ground, red eyed holding a celestial silver sword in her hands.

"I refuse to tolerate anymore," Was all she said before she plunged the sword straight through my chest.

Flashback Over

"Evangeline?"

I turned to see Ava still inside the dome but now standing up at the edge of it with her hand pressed up against it as she stared at us with wide eyes.

"Avangeline?" I asked as I approached the dome with my hand up against it.

She flinched rather hard as her eyes flashed red for a moment.

"Eve I can hear you but I can't see you, everything is just gold and blurry," She panicked as she looked around in confusion.

"Ava calm down and don't worry, we will figure all of this out and we will get you out," I said calmly.

Chapter 17.

Eva's POV

She banged on the dome as a fearful expression began to arise on her face.

"Eve please get me out," She pleaded as she continued to bang.

I walked up to the dome as a dagger materialized in my hand, I attempted to stab through the dome but as my dagger made contact I felt a painful electric current run through my body as Ava screamed and I was thrown backwards.

"What just happened?" Ariel asked as she helped me up.

"Her mind has created a barrier to block out any and all outside distractions," Zachary said.

"To protect herself?" I asked as I rubbed the back of my head.

"No, to protect us,"

"WHO IS ELIZABETH?!" Ava screamed out as she held her head tightly, eyes glowing even brighter.

"Ava is an Angel of mind manipulation, of course her mind would be too powerful to just have a door simply locked," Zachary whispered.

"Why do you keep talking about locking doors? Weren't you just supposed to erase a memory?" I asked annoyed.

"Our minds are filled with-"

Zachary was cut off by a screaming Ava.

"WHO IS DEREK?!" She cried out as she slid down the dome.

"Why are you just standing there while your mate is in pain?" Ariel questioned, looking at Derek.

Taylor came running outside as she attempted to latch onto Derek but he growled at her as he snatched his arm away from her.

"If you can't do anything what makes you think I can?!" He asked surprised.

"You're her mate!" I yelled out.

He studied me for a moment before walking up to the dome. He placed his hand directly onto it causing her screaming to finally stop.

Maybe this was working.

She slowly stood up as she stared directly at Derek, wide eyed.

"Avangeline?" Derek asked.

Her wide gold eyes soon began to shift to a blood red color, a color not many had the luxury of seeing because the moment you saw an Angel with blood red eyes, you were pronounced dead.

"You killed her," She whispered towards Derek.

I walked up beside Derek as I placed my hand on the dome.

"What did you say Ava?" I asked even though I heard her words perfectly clear.

"HE KILLED HER!!!" She screamed as she raised her celestial sword.

She swung at the dome, hoping it would do some kind of damage but the sword merely bounced back, no damage to be seen.

"Why isn't it breaking?" I asked, relieved that Derek's head was still intact.

"It's like her mind and her body are two separate beings right now, her body is running off of her emotions and her mind is is protecting us while things are patched together and they both can finally connect as one again," Zachary explained.

Ava's wings began to retract from her back as she began attacking the dome with her wings but not even a scratch could be seen.

She screamed and as she did, flames shot from her mouth , onto the dome as we all stood there in shock, a power we've never seen before and I'm sure a power she didn't know she was capable of.

"So what do we do now?" I asked after a moment of silence except for Ava's screams in the background.

"Maybe Ava wasn't the danger that the Moon Goddess meant when she called us all here," Eli suggested.

"Alpha Liam," I said out loud.

"There hasn't been any signs of Liam anywhere, he died years ago when Ava took his life," Ariel rolled her eyes.

"So you're calling me a liar?" Derek growled.

"Not a liar just paranoid," Ariel said sweetly.

"Well Ava did say there was an attack on the white wolf pack, that could have something to do with Liam," Is rugged my shoulders, throwing suggestions out.

"So you want to believe that Liam is alive?" Ariel asked, unconvinced.

"Yeah so I can kick his ass for hurting my sister, he left a permanent scar on her." I said.

Silence took over the group as everyone looked over at me.

Finally Alpha Derek was the one to break the silence.

"What do you mean a permanent scar? Emotionally?"

I shook my head.

"Emotionally and physically,"

"Physically?" He asked.

"She has the word weak carved into her skin on her lower back," Zachary pointed out.

"She shows no one and she doesn't talk about it because it still haunts her, whenever she hears that word she's just reminded of him she she feels as though she has to prove herself," I explained.

"A haunted soul," Derek said lowly to himself as we all looked over to see Ava with silver axes in her hands, trying to smash at the dome.

"Why did she care so much for the vampire?" He asked.

"Derek it doesn't matter, that thing tried to kill you and if it wasn't for me you might have died," Taylor pleaded.

"It was a child it wouldn't have killed me, I want to know why she was so special to her," Derek insisted as he stared at her with annoyance.

"Elizabeth was like a daughter to her, she finally had someone who loved her automatically and never rejected her. IN some way we all have rejected Avangeline and still harbor the guilt inside of us," I said as I hung my head low.

"Ava was the weakest of us all and she was a disgrace to all Angels so when she began her new rank some of us became jealous and others downright rejected her," Eli said as he rubbed the back of his neck.

" I always wanted to killer her for being the weakest Angel fo us all to being the most powerful," Ariel said quietly.

"And she relayed us all for it. It was twenty against one and we all lost, the only thing that calmed her down was the Moon Goddess herself," Zachary admitted.

We looked over and noticed Ava staring at us, eyes no longer glowing but now there tearful light brown eyes. As she gently placed her hand on the dome it whisked away as if it never existed in the first place.

"She was the only person I ever truly received unconditional love from without a price. From the moment she looked at me she thought of me as her mother, her protector and her safe space without having to use my body, my mind, my soul or my rank. She loved me for me and she repaired my broken heart," Ava choked out.

She turned around as she lifted her shirt to expose int red lettering engraved into her lower back which read 'weak', each letter in bold and still looked fresh.

"He did that to me one night when he tied me down, feels like it was yesterday but it had to be decades ago. I didn't have any strength or energy to fight back so I was forced to endured it while he scraped to the bone," She shuddered in disgust at the memory.

She closed her eyes as she took a deep breath.

"I, Avangeline reject you, Derek-"

Derek quickly rushed over as he slapped his hand over her mouth to silence her as he growled.

He whispered something into her ear which caused her to collapse in his arms and break down crying. He picked her up bridal style as he stuck his face in the crook of her neck and carried her off to the pack house.

"What do you think he whispered to her?" I asked.

"Something about Elizabeth, she's the only one that's able to get there like this, Elizabeth and Liam," Ariel said.

I looked over to my left and noticed Zachary beside me frowning.

"What's your deal?" I questioned him.

"He doesn't deserve her," He frowned.

"But you do?" I snorted.

"I have done nothing but treat her the way she deserves to be treated," He huffed.

"Even if that's true there's nothing you can do. The mate bond within wolves is a sacred bond that the Moon Goddess conjured up herself, they will never be able to let go of each other, they own a piece of each other's souls and they are intertwined. Once she finds out who Nicholas's mate is it's best that no one else complicates the picture," I suggested.

"Unfortunately there is one person who still has a hold on her heart and I can see it, the same fucked up bitch that did this to her, that scarred her and still owns her. A person she just refuses to let go of," He said angrily as he began walking away.

"And who is that?" I asked, already knowing the answer to that.

He turned back to look at me.

"Alpha Liam,"

Chapter 18.

Ava POV

Life has a funny way of reminding you just how mortal you once were. The only difference between us was the duration of our lives and how much we could endure, despite those things we weren't much different. They say the Moon Goddess made us in her likeness, given a life that was not meant to have so did I truly appreciate the live that I was given?

The answer was simple.

Yes.

To feel heartbreak, to feel pain, to feel love and be loved.

That's what it meant to be alive in this world.

I was currently in the Blood Moon pack house in a bedroom that Derek brought me in. The moment he laid me down he immediately left to give me space to recollect all of my thoughts. After Derek whispered into my ear that he wasn't the one that killed Elizabeth for some reason I broke down, I sensed with true sincerity in his heart and mind, because I can read minds, that he honestly did not kill her.

It was Taylor, whom I would deal with later.

I spent so much energy trying to murder him for something he didn't do, blaming him for my love lost but if it weren't for the other Angels I would have lost two of my loves in one day.

Love.

Did I love Alpha Derek?

Everyday the pull felt stronger and stronger despite our missteps but yet, this was no where near worse than Alpha Liam.

Of course I would able to disintegrate Taylor for not only marking what was mine but also killing another I love.

I heard a knock on the door and as I sat up there revealed a very concerned looking Alpha Derek.

He stepped inside and closed the door behind him as he noticed I was awake. He cleared his throat as he sat on the bed with hesitance in his aura.

"Are you alright? This has been a wild couple of days," He said as he finally broke the silence.

"I've been better, you should try being in my head it's honestly a mess," I muttered as I rubbed my forehead.

"Well it's good that you're safe from yourself and feeling better, maybe some rest will make you feel better," Derek suggested.

"No I have to finish my mission, it's still ingrained into my brain so therefore the mission isn't complete," I urged.

"Why don't you rest for just a day or two before you and then me and the other Angels can worry about Liam," Derek said sternly.

"What the fuck do I look like allowing the other lower ranking Angels to finish a job while the Black winged Assassin Angel rests in bed because she's feeling a little down?" I said flabbergasted as I looked at him with confusion.

I noticed a twinkle of amusement sparkle in his eyes as he looked at me.

"You just got mind fucked, you attempted to kill me after your vampire child died, temporarily had your memory erased but somehow your mind was able to repair them as you went through an explosive episode in the middle of some protective bubble? I think that's more than feeling a little down," He explained with squinted eyes.

"Sounds like a normal Tuesday to me," I shrugged my shoulders as I grinned.

"You Angels are insane, and I was just lucky enough to be the mate of one," He muttered as he slightly chuckled.

Silence overtook us for a moment as he looked out of the window and I studied his face.

He was a very attractive man, more mature than when you usually find your mate but time was irrelevant to me for I was centuries old. A werewolf and Angel pairing always confused me because no matter what I did my mate would always die before me since I could not die, only under certain circumstances. Was I just destined to watch my mate die of old age as I continued to live on in heartbreak?

Was this what the Moon Goddess wished upon me?

"So you really won't listen to me and rest for a couple days?" I heard Derek ask me.

"I listen to no one but the Moon Goddess herself...not even my mate unfortunately," I stuck my tongue out.

"Seems like you would listen to Alpha Nicholas," He mumbled to himself but I caught every word.

"Don't bring him up now or ever again, end of discussion," I growled.

More silence fell between us as he looked down at his hands, obviously something bothering him.

"Ava I am truly sorry for how things have turned out, none of this was intentional," I looked up and noticed he gesturing to the mark on his neck.

"It's fine...do you love her?" I asked.

"Taylor? No I never loved Taylor, we just became comfortable with each other, I'm 29 years old, I thought I would never find my mate so I selfishly kept Taylor by my side to eventually become my Luna if I never found my mate, 11 years later here we are," He smiled at me as he looked me deep in my eyes.

"Wow...you really are a loser," I smiled as I leaned forward towards him.

"Takes a loser to know one you omega," He jokingly said as he too leaned forward, caressing the side of my face with his hand before pulling me in and gently pressing his lips against mine. Tingling sensations began to erupt all over me as a wave of euphoria washed over me, bringing me ease and enjoyment as his finger tips caressed every inch of skin that he could, our lips moving in sync as our lips glided together with ease. I felt his tongue glide across my bottom lip gently, requesting access and I opened my mouth to grant him such access.

His lips felt as though they belonged, like there was no other place for them except on my body, like it would be a crime to put those lips anywhere else. except for here.

I moaned lightly as he laid me back against the bed, climbing on top of me with his muscular arms on either side of my head before breaking away ever so lightly and looking down at me with lust in his eyes.

"We have a problem," He said with slight ragged breath.

"What's the problem?" I asked curiously.

"Well I want to fuck you right here and right now but I can't because of this mark, it would seriously hurt Taylor due to her putting her claim on me," He explained.

"Hurt her I don't care," I urged as I pulled him closer as my hands began to travel down his torso, causing him to shiver in delight.

"Fuck Ava, right now I need to focus on a way to get this mark off of me," He said as he crawled away from me and stood up from the bed.

That bitch deserves pain.

"Maybe you also want to regroup with your Angel pals?" He said as he made his way towards the door.

"Fine, but we will be continuing this dilemma later," I scolded as he chuckled and walked to the door.

I gathered myself for a moment before I walked out of the room and headed outside where I noticed Eve hanging up in a tree, Zachary chasing Ariel around in the sky and Eli laying in the grass as he looked dup at the clouds.

Once Eve noticed me she immediately flew down towards me with a concerned face.

"I need to train," I said sternly as she approached me.

"Are you sure?" She questioned, but she knew I've been through worse.

I nodded my head and she immediately put a protective shield around us, enclosing the two of us as Zachary, Ariel and Eli circled around to watch us closely.

"I don't want to go easy on you so are you sure you're ready to train so quickly?" She questioned once more.

I nodded my head as I rolled my eyes.

A smirked form at the corners of her mouth as her eyes began to glow a bright golden, daggers appearing in her hand as she launched one at me with top speed, almost striking my shoulder. I dodged out of the way as I quickly summoned my bow and arrow, launching a silver arrow at her, missing her face by inches as she swerved away from it. She flapped her wings as strong as she could creating a strong gust of wind, knocking into the shield.

I screamed as fire shot out of my mouth, scaring Eve even though it burned my throat badly. She knocked the fire with her wings and as she uncovered herself I quickly shot am arrow straight into her chest causing her to fall right to her knees.

He eyes immediately stopped glowing as she looked down at the arrow angrily.

"Fine you win, I'm dead," She said annoyed as she pulled the arrow straight from her chest.

I grinned proudly as she took the protective dome down.

Zachary walked up to me and shook his head disapproving.

"It's good to see that you're in better health but you are one of the best when it comes to physical training, mental training is what you need to steady your mind and find the cause of your issues.

"How do I do that?" I asked.

As Eve walked away from us Zachary created another protective shield around us, much more intImate with nothing but darkness surrounding us. I looked around worriedly until I was able to see the golden glow of Zachary's wings.

We sat down cross legged in front of each other, feeling his breath slightly fan against my cheek as I looked him in the eyes.

"Are you sure you want to do this training? This is something extremely deep that involves you seeing things you might not want to see," Zachary warned.

I had to get strong, I had to defeat the demons in my mind if I were to come face to face with the true monster.

"Press your thumbs on my temples in my head as you wrap your hands around my head and Ill do the same," He instructed.

I did as I was told and immediately his eyes began to turn bright gold as I felt myself slipping into darkness, no longer able to see Zachary in front of me, almost as if I was falling.

We were entering my mind.

Chapter 19.

Ava POV (A/N they are inside Ava's mind so ya enjoy!)

I walked around in this dark empty abyss, looking for a sign of life in this lonely darkness I was unfamiliar with.

"Follow the sound of my voice Ava," I heard the sound of Zachary's voice behind me.

I turned around and immediately began running towards the sound of his voice until I felt myself slam straight a solid figure, I looked up as I rubbed my head to see Zachary's glowing face staring down at me with a smile, as he outstretched his wings to shine light for us. I stepped back as I looked around and was still greeted by eerie darkness.

"Where are we?" I asked him.

He looked at me with a bored expression, almost as if I were supposed to know where we were.

"We are inside of your mind Ava, the part that holds memories, most people have forgotten and others that the mind has blocked out for traumatic reasons. I am the Angel of mind manipulation but only memory so the past is what we will look into for you," He explained.

"Why does my head seem so empty?" I shrugged my shoulders.

He chuckled.

"I haven't done anything yet love," He raised his arms as his eyes began to glow, suddenly doors began to appear along walls, one by one as dimly lit candles appeared next to them.

"This one is promising, let's go through this one," He pointed to the dark oak door in front of as as he began to walk towards it.

"Wait," I said as I pulled against his arm causing him to stop and look at me.

"Where do all of these doors lead to?" I asked.

He smiled.

"These are all doorways into your memories, you don't know what's behind each door because you can only see the present and what's in front of you but my power allows me to see what's behind each door so you have to have faith in me," He said as he intertwined my hand in his and pulled me forward.

He slowly opened the door and immediately I was blinded by a bright light.

I looked around and found myself standing in a field of flowers with Zachary by my side.

I looked ahead and noticed myself sitting in the middle of the field as I held up a small Elizabeth in my hands.

"Zachary is that-"

"Yes it's you and Elizabeth when she was a bit smaller. I wanted to show you this specific memory because you said some things that really stuck to me and I think they are worth remembering," He said.

"Mommy I wanna go higher!" Elizabeth squealed.

She had a small tinted shield around her small form to prevent her fragile skin from burning in the sun.

"A little later Ellie, I'm just tired," The past me said as I placed her down in my lap.

She pouted softly as she looked up at me with big wide eyes, looking at me with such admiration.

"Mommy why is this around me?" She asked a she pointed at the shield around her.

"To protect you from the sun, you aren't like mommy but that doesn't mean I won't stop loving you," I said as I held her tightly.

"What happens when you die?" Ellie asked as she held a flower in her small fist.

"Well you go off with the Moon Goddess," Was all I said.

It seemed as though I was in a deep thought.

"I don't want to die," Ellie argued as she gripped the flower tightly in her hand until the petals crumbled.

"Everyone dies Elizabeth, no matter how much you don't want it to happen or how much you try to stall it, it will always happen. But those hurt by death the most are not the ones that die, it's the loved ones. They mourn, they grow depressed or they want to die themselves to join you but we all have to remember that when someone dies they never truly leave you, they will be with you, watching over you,"

I pointed to Elizabeth's chest.

"And in here,"

"It's the love and the memories that count!" Elizabeth giggled.

"Exactly!" I said as I smiled.

I walked up to the pair as a single tear slid down my face, reaching down to gently caress Elizabeth's face but sadly my hand went right through her.

"Ava this is a memory, you can't interfere with it no matter what. I'm sorry love," Zachary said as he placed his hand on my shoulder.

"No it's fine, I just needed to see her one last time happy and smiling and I have to remember my own words. Elizabeth is still watching over me and in my heart," I smiled as I wiped away at my face.

Another door appeared next to us as Zachary grabbed my hand and led me through the door, a much darker memory as I felt a sense of dread in my stomach.

"Why do you keep doing this to me?" I heard a voice call out in the darkness.

"What is this?" I asked as I looked dup at Zachary.

"This is a memory you won't like," He frowned as we continued walking.

"Because you are nothing but a toy to me," I heard a husky voice from the distance that still seemed to send shivers down my spine, even in a memory.

As we approached closer a dim light appeared, this time we were in a bedroom, a very younger self of me was sitting on the bed balled up as a Alpha Liam stood against the wall, staring at me with a bored expression.

He was a tall man, easily over six foot with sparkling green eyes I was always hypnotized by and dirty blonde hair. He had his signature cut on his face that started from the bottom of his right eyelid to the bottom of his jaw on the left side of his face thanks to me.

"How can you say that to me?" I asked angrily. I looked so pitiful and weak with my hair so short and uneven, the dullness of my brown eyes that read nothing but sadness and hopeless thoughts. I noticed my wings were out and fluttered, a sight I never wanted to see again. Small grey wings that barely reached either wall of the room as they slightly drooped, how I was able to even fly was an amazement.

Liam shrugged his shoulders.

"I'm speaking nothing but the truth, you're nothing but a toy to me. I definitely don't need a Luna by my side and if I didn't it definitely wouldn't be you, I refuse to let others see you as my mate," He said disgusted.

"But I'm your mate, you're supposed to love and protect me, love only me and no one else. If you crave love then I can give it all to you, if you need someone to listen then I am all ears, if you want someone to please you then my body is all yours," I screamed at him as I began to cry.

Such a painful memory to watch.

I watched as anger flickered in his eyes.

"You just don't understand do you Avangeline? I never wanted a mate, especially someone like you," He growled.

"Why do you treat me as if I'm such a dirty shame? I'm just an Angel that's starting out. Why can't you just love me Liam? You seek all this love from other women and you enjoy the attention and the fact that everyone falls for doubt you can't even see that you constantly hurt me everyday, physically and emotionally but I can't stand to leave you," I cried out.

I felt so sorry for myself, a day I couldn't forget, a time that I hated. Begging a man for his love, not sticking up for myself and accepting this abuse.

Liam quickly stalked over to the bed as he back handed me, the echo sounding around the room as I fell to the bed.

"Who the fuck are you to tell me what I enjoy and what I shouldn't enjoy? You are nothing but my property bitch and the Moon Goddess knows that. Suck it the fuck up and deal with it because guess what? You don't have the courage or heart to leave me so it looks like you're stuck with me," He grinned darkly.

He hovered over me as he punched me square in the face and growled angrily as the bones quickly healed.

"Who the fuck is Avon?!" He roared in my face, his possessive side beginning to take over.

"I don't know!" I cried out as I tried to escape from his grasp but he quickly grabbed my arm and threw me across the room.

"Don't you dare lie to me! I heard you at night calling his name! Who the fuck is he?!" He roared once more as he grabbed me by the throat and slammed me against the wall.

I kicked my feet out in pain but it was no use. My face began turning red and then purple as he began pressing his thumbs into my throat and before I knew it I saw my eyes roll to the back of my head and I stopped all movement, flopping to the floor as he let go of me.

"I have to find a way to get you out of my life without ending my own life," He spat as he looked down at me on the ground.

Liam turned to me and looked me directly in my eyes as if he could see me standing in place and smiled.

"Who is Avon?" He asked.

My head erupted into a massive headache as I fell to the floor.

"Ava what's wrong?" I heard Zachary ask above me.

The walls and floor around us began to shake violently as I felt something pull me by the back of my collar and force us out of this current memory. We were back in the corridor but this time I looked up to see a giant black door with a silver doorknob and a giant red X on the front of it. I stood up as I examined it, something pulling me to open it almost like it was calling for me.

"What's behind this door?" I asked.

"I-I don't know, it's. like something is preventing me from seeing anything past this door," Zach said worriedly.

I began walking towards the door as I placed my hand on the surprisingly warm silver knob.

"Ava I'm not so sure-"

The door immediately swung open and I was forced through the doorway, I looked behind me to Zachary Zachary trying to take a step forward but was forced back into the darkness.

"AVA!" He screamed. I tried running back to the entrance but the door was closed in my face.

Only silence and darkness surrounded me.

Chapter 20.

Zachary POV

I opened my eyes and watched as the protective shield around us began to disappear. I looked in front of my to see Ava still in front of me but her hands were now in her lap and her eyes were still glowing bright gold.

I was so confused.

What just happened? What was the memory and why didn't it allow for me to see it?

"Zachary!" I heard a yell behind me. I turned around to see a very concerned Eve and Alpha Derek running towards me, trying to figure out what was happening.

"What's going on? Why is she still sitting there with her eyes all glowing?" Alpha Derek questioned.

"Her mind has kicked me and and apparently wants to show her something only she is allowed to see," I shrugged my shoulders as I stood up, dusting the dirt from my back side.

"What was so secretive that her mind had to show her and not you? Your power is seeing into the past for Goddess sake!" Eve said irritated.

"I don't know! I was forced out and she was forced in and that's all I have to say about that," I growled in annoyance.

I noticed as Derek walked over to Ava and picked her up bridal style, arms flopping to her side as she nuzzled into his neck.

"Just make sure you make it back Avangeline," He whispered into her ear.

I watched as her body shivered and flinched when he said her full name. Something had to be wrong id her body reacted this way even when is was unconscious.

"Eva what's the reason for Avangeline hating her full name?" I called out.

Out of the corner of my eye I noticed she flinched so badly in Derek's arms that heroes flashed red as she flinched so badly, he nearly dropped her.

"I'm going to lay her down so she can calm down," Alpha Derek insisted as he advanced towards the pack house. I watched Ava's beautiful figure in his arms as she cuddled into his chest, relaxed by the touch of her mate due to the mate pull.

It saddened me that I could possibly lose Ava forever because she truly belonged to her mate.

I turned around to noticed Eve eyeing me very closely, as if curious.

"Ava told me that it still hurts because it reminds her of when Liam called her that and ten abused her," She explained slowly, still eyeing me closely.

I shook my head and sighed.

"For her to have the reaction it's not enough and I think she doesn't even know the real reason. I think it may have something to do with her mortal self, almost like an instinct whenever someone says her name to just expect pain. She's just making up excuses to fill in the gaps.

"If you're so smart why didn't you foretell that her being with both you and Nicholas would mess her up?" Eve glared at me.

"I can only see the past, I can't see into the future, no one truly can," I sighed.

She mumbled something to herself, something that even I couldn't hear as she took off into the sky with her white wings flapping beside her. She reminded me so much of her sister, so free spirited and out spoken.

I decided to go and visit Ava to make sure she was okay as I walked into the pack house. As I may my way up to the second floor I heard hushed voices behind one of the doors.

"After everything we've been through, you're really choosing her?"

"It's not that simple and you know it, I told you if I never found my mate then you would be my Luna but I've found her and I can't and won't abandon her,"

"She was never there for you, I was always there for you all these years,"

"And I will always appreciate it no matter what but what we had was comfortable, that's all,"

"I see the way you look at her, the way you've never looked at me before. With so much love, lust and admiration, it's like I don't even exist anymore,"

"I'm sorry Taylor maybe there's a chance-"

"Don't you dare finish that sentence! Let me stay in pain for the rest of my life because of my rejection while you go off all happy and in love. For fucks sake they slept together!"

"My mate has been through so much over the years, for however long she has lived. Don't drag her into this mess just because she didn't know Nicholas rejected you for her, she was oblivious,"

"And what makes you think she isn't still in love with him?"

There was a silence in the room for a moment.

"Get out," I heard a low growl.

The door swung open revealing a teary eyed Taylor. She looked up at me with surprise before briskly walking away.

I entered the office where I noticed Alpha Derek with his head in his hands behind his desk, that's when I cleared my throat.

HIs head shot up and he immediately growled at me.

"What do you want Angel?" He growled.

I put my hands up in surrender as I shook my head.

"We need to go see the white wolves," I admitted.

"I don't want to see those people, especially that Alpha," He huffed.

"There's a chance that we might be able to get rid of that nasty mark on your neck if Nicholas decides to take Taylor back, besides we need to start looking more into Liam without any other casualties," I argued.

He folded his hands together as he closed his eyes, deep in thought about the situation.

"How would Nicholas taking Taylor back make this mark go away?" He questioned.

"Once Taylor marks her true mate the mark will fade from your neck, as if it never happened," I explained.

"Give me second to think about it," He said as he shooed me away. I nodded my head as I lightly chuckled, the gesture reminded me so much of Ava.

I walked out of the room and set on a mission to do what I originally came into this house to do.

I looked through every room and knocked on every door until I came across Ava tucked into a room as if she were sleeping peacefully, I closed the door behind me as I walked up to the bed to examine her.

"Avangeline," I whispered into her ear.

She flinched once more as her eyes quickly flashed red before returning to normal. If only I knew why her name triggered such a reaction then maybe I could be able to help. Or maybe that was what she was going to heal on her own.

"Avon," She said out loud.

I looked at her in confusion before looking around the room.

Who was Avon?

"Who is Avon?" I heard a voice behind me.

I turned around to see Derek staring at me from the doorway.

"I have no idea, in a memory Liam questioned her about saying that same name in her sleep," I shrugged.

"Sounds like something I should be concerned about. I decided that I'll go to the white wolf pack," He announced.

"Well that was a fast thought process," I smirked.

I wasn't an idiot, he wanted to get Taylor out of the picture and that mark off of his neck so he could truly be together with Ava.

"I can set up a couple cars-"

I shook my head.

"No we are flying, it's much faster. I'll carry Avangeline, Eli can carry Taylor and either Eve or Ariel can carry you,"

He snorted with laughter as he shook his head.

"I refuse to ride on the back of an Angel. I can run just as fast, I have white wolf blood in me," He rolled his eyes.

I smirked as I leaned against the wall.

"Trust me, flying on one of our backs is so much faster. You'll only lose a little bit of your dignity," I smirked.

"Don't test me Angel," He said lowly.

I smiled as I walked out of the room past him as I shook my head. When I reached outside I noticed Eli, Ariel and Eve crowded out front as they looked at me.

"So what's your plan?" Eve crossed her arms.

"You'll see when we get there," I said, raising my eyebrows.

I noticed Derek walking out with Ava in his arms and Taylor trailing along right behind him.

"How nice of you to tell the others about my plan without even asking first," I said irritated.

"Anything for you pal," He smiled in my face as he passed Ava to Eve instead of me.

"Derek I'm not going, I don't want to see him," She crossed her arms as she huffed.

"TAYLOR!" Derek shouted out in his Alpha tone causing her to whimper and then bow.

"Good, now go with the other girl," He pointed to Ariel who groaned in annoyance.

"And how are you getting there?" Eve asked.

"Running in wolf form,"

She snorted.

"Good luck with that,"

She dashed up into the sky with Ava in her arms and began to fly south.

"Hop on and make sure you hold on tight," Ariel winked at Taylor.

The moment Taylor was secure, Ariel took off full speed into the sky with Taylor screaming behind her.

Alpha Derek shifted into his midnight black wolf white white fur on his back and took off into the forest, into the direction of the white wolf pack.

"Eli, while their Alpha is gone you need to make sure nothing happens to this pack, especially with Liam possibly out there," I instructed.

He nodded at me and I immediately took off into the sky.

Chapter 21

Zachary POV

2 hours later

I managed to catch up to Eve in the sky as I still noticed Ava who seemed as though she was peacefully sleeping and nodded at her.

She nodded back and glared at me.

"What is your problem with me?" I roared over the sound of the wind.

"I see the way you look at her still, hoping she will get back with you and abandon everyone for you, she doesn't need that manipulation in her life!" She snapped.

I rolled my eyes.

"Get over it! I can admire her all hat I want but I now know my place with her so I'll continue to admire from afar! It's not manipulation it's love,"

"How about you-" All of a sudden something zoomed straight into Eve causing her to spin out of control and drop Ava.

"AVA!!!" SHE SCREAMED.

Avangeline was one of the best flyers in the group, she was able to maneuver herself in ways we just couldn't and understand her speed, wing control and resistance. Ariel was the second best while Eve, Eli and I were better at landing.

I quickly grabbed Taylor from Ariel's back and she immediately zoomed down, going almost as fast as the speed of sound as she managed to grab Ava and realized she wouldn't have time to slow herself down in enough time at the speed she was falling. She clutched the back of Ava's head as she flipped her, her back now facing the ground, and prepared to crash land.

She screamed loudly on impact as she smacked into the ground and took most of the impact as her body began to re heal slowly but surely.

Eve and I zoomed down with Taylor on my back and as we gently landed we raced over towards the two and I grabbed Ava out of Ariel's hands so that Eve could help her up.

She seemed fine, just a bit shaken up.

"Ariel are you alright?" I asked.

She looked up as she glared at Eve.

"What the fuck was that? You just lose control for no reason and drop your own sister?" She yelled.

"Something smacked into me! It was coming so fast I couldn't even see what it was!" Eve shouted back.

"Evangeline?" We all looked over to see Alpa Nicholas staring at us with wide eyes.

Eve ran over to him and gave him a bone crushing hug, him returning the action.

He noticed me and glared at me for a split second before he noticed a motionless Ava in my arms and it almost looked as if he were ready to burst into tears.

He walked over towards me and gently grabbed her out of my arms.

"What's wrong with her?" He whispered.

"She's stuck in a coma like state but more so stuck in her head," I said.

He looked down at her face before gently planting a kiss onto her lips, simultaneously causing two very powerful growls around us.

We all turned in surprise to see Taylor and Derek standing there with pitch black eyes and faces full of envy and jealousy.

Nicholas's face turned white as his eyes landed upon Taylor.

Derek stalked towards Nicholas as dirt and mud covered his bare chest and he growled in Nicholas's face, slightly towering over him.

Such an amusing sight.

"Don't you dare touch her again," He growled dangerously.

"What the fuck is going on here?" Nicholas asked annoyed and furious.

"We've come here to find answers to many conflicts, one of them being hat your secret is out and that Taylor is your true mate," I said as I motioned to Taylor.

Derek snatched Ava from his arms as he stalked towards the pack house to make sure she was safe, Nicholas looking at all of us with annoyance.

"Nicholas what happened to the protective shield Ava put up?" Eve asked as she noticed just how close the pack house was to us.

He shrugged his shoulders.

"It just went away,"

"Must have went away when Ava got trapped in her own mind,"

I watched out of the corner of my eye as Taylor looked at Nicholas with such sadness before stalking away from the group, obviously conflicted.

"I don't want her," Nicholas said once he realized she was out of ear shot.

"That's such a horrible and asshole thing to say," Eve scrunched up her nose.

"I love Ava too much to let her go," He sighed.

"But Ava will end up letting you go," Eve said irritated.

"No she won't I refuse to believe that," He growled.

"As much as I don't want to admit this but they are attracted to each other, their mate bond is growing stronger and stronger, the only thing holding Derek back is that mark on his neck but I can feel the connection between the two," I snorted.

He turned to me and glared.

"No one asked you bitch," He growled.

I was taken aback by his hostility towards me but I couldn't blame him for hating me, I did for in fact take the one he loved away from him.

"Nicholas you wouldn't be able to stay with her anyway, being in love with an Angel just isn't that simple. We live for eternity, you would just die and leave her alone," Eve said in a saddened tone.

"So how the fuck do you explain the relationship between her and her mate, he would just die and leave her alone too since he's just a wolf," He in a 'duh' tone.

"I'm not sure but the Moon Goddess has a plan for everything,"

"I still don't want Taylor," He crossed his arms over his chest.

"You need a Luna for you pack," I said annoyed now.

"And Ava was perfect," He insisted.

I was beginning to grow hot with anger as Nicholas looked at me with such disgust and annoyance, his hot headedness was beginning to annoy me.

"Just take your fucking mate!" I yelled at him.

"He looked shocked for a moment as he processed my words and growled back at me.

"The only true mate that is mine is Avangeline," He insisted.

There was a loud roar from behind us as Derek came storming up to us in a fit of rage, eyes as black as the ocean during the night.

"She is mine and only mine!" He roared as he approached us.

"She doesn't want you she wants me!" Nicholas argued.

"Nicholas just back down!" Eve yelled out.

Out of no where a large figure came and rammed into Nicholas flying across the lawn. We all stood in shock as we stared at the stranger. He was about over 6 foot tall with dirty blonde hair and vibrant green that seemed to sparkle in the sun, he had a long scar from the bottom of his right eye lid all the way down to the bottom right side of his jaw.

He stood up slowly with a smirk across his face with his hand sin his pockets and his large black wings spread out before us. These weren't like Ava's beautiful pure black, bird like velvety Angel wings. They were a tad bit smaller and reminded me of bat wings with rough leather like skin in between each joint and bone.

He was an archangel. Archangels belonged in the underworld under the care of a different group of Angels, it wasn't our job to deal with arch angels, we were only assassins. So why did I have a feeling we had to take out this specific one?

As he smirked at Eve I noticed that he seemed oddly familiar.

"You know, for being fraternal twins you both sure do look alike," He grinned at Eve.

Alpha Liam in the flesh.

"Li-L-Lia,+ Eve stuttered but just couldn't get the words out.

"Alpha Liam," I said darkly.

He turned to me with a genuine smile on his face.

"It's a pleasure to meet you and my apologizes but I don't think we've ever met. Your name is?" He asked politely.

"Zachary, gold ranked assassin Angel and server of the Divine Moon Goddess herself," I said tall and proudly.

"An assassin Angel huh? Is Ava still that same pitiful low ranking Angel? I'd be surprised if the Moon Goddess found her useful for anything," He asked with a laugh.

"Avangeline is-" Eve started to say but I shook my head at her.

It was obvious that Liam was unaware of who Ava truly was now.

"I'm glad you found us so I can personally rip your fucking head off," Derek growled.

Liam turned to him with a surprise as he slightly bowed.

"Alpha Derek! It's an honor to be in the presence of an Alpha of the same... how do you say it? Of the same rank? Status? Vicious and cold blooded killers? Top of the rank? It's been a decade since another Alpha like me came around," He smiled genuinely.

Derek looked at him with such a cold expression, I wasn't sure who was more intimidating, Liam or Derek.

"I don't we are on the same status since I'm not known as a man who beats his mate senseless for fun," Derek growled.

Anger flashed in Liam's eyes as he took his hands out of his pockets and cracked his knuckles. His charming façade was beginning to to wash away.

"And why would that bitch tell you something like that?" He asked angrily.

"Watch how you address her!" Derek roared, shaking us all to our cores.

Liam studied him for a moment as he lightly smirked.

"You're her second chance mate aren't you?" He frowned.

"Wasn't expecting something like that? Look around you, all of these males have slept with your ex mate, touching the same parts you laid your hands on and claimed!" Derek laughed as he gestured to Nicholas and I.

He was trying to switch the role and gain the upper hand by digging under his skin and Derek was enjoying it.

"That fucking whore, he belongs to me and only me! I own that bitch and now we can be together forever," Liam raised his hands.

"You own nothing," Derek said darkly.

Liam's eyes began to glow a bright red as large flaming chains began to materialize in his hands, burning the grass around him. His hands began to turn as black as charcoal from the flames, to withstand the heat.

Derek shifted into his black and white wolf as he snarled into Liam's direction.

Before we could do anything Liam charged at Derek but a scream filled the air as we all held our ears in pain. Liam was tackled to the ground by a dark brooding figure, that figure was none other than Ava herself.

She stood up.

Her silver bow and arrow now in her hands as her red eyes beamed at Liam's fallen figure.

"You shall no longer have control over my mind or my life," She said as she outstretched her giant black wings, Liam watching her in amazement.

Chapter 22.

A va POV

(We are going back a little in the story to when the door closed on her in her mind, to show you the memories and why they were so important.)

I grabbed the handle of the door and tried to use all of the strength I had in my body but it was no use, it just wouldn't budge. I banged on the door as I screamed, ultimately giving up and pressing my back against the door as I slid down it.

"What do you want from me?!" I screamed out to nothingness.

"Wait up Avangeline!" I heard the small voice of a little boy.

I immediately stood up as I looked around at the darkness.

"Hello? I called out.

A small light brown mousy haired boy with sweet freckles and baby blue eyes appeared before me as if he were glowing.

Avangeline come on, you're so slow," He giggled as he ran away.

For some reason this boy seemed so familiar.

He began running towards the light so I had no choice but to follow him.

I ran through the light after the little boy until a pack territory came into view. It was a beautiful sight. It was a smaller wolf pack than usual populations, there was a field with all k=different kind of wild flowers bloomed everywhere and little children ran around playing with each other or their families as shifted wolves pounced on each other and played.

"Avangeline!" The same boy called out to me.

Just then a small little girl with honey brown eyes and jet black curly hair and the cutest smile popped her head out from under a bush.

"I'm right here Avon!" She giggled as she climbed out of the bushes.

The little boy pouted.

"Don't run away from me,"

"You still never found Evangeline!" The girl screamed.

Just then another little girl with similar appearance appeared as she huffed. It was obvious that these two were sisters, twins even.

He didn't even bother looking for me! That's because he likes you!" Little Eve pouted.

"Eww Avon you can't like me, that's gross but we have to stay friend thought," Little Ava giggled.

So Avon was an old childhood friend, I couldn't understand why he was so important.

A door appeared right beside me so I decided to enter it, this must be my minds way of leading me out of here so I guess I had no choice but to follow it. I was outside again but this time in front of me were the same two children as before but this time they looked to be about young teenagers. It was a dark and starry night as the two teens were laying in that same field as they looked dup at the stars.

"Avon do you like me?" I asked as I laid down beside him on the ground just looking up at the stars.

"Is it that obvious?" He sighed beside her.

"A little but it's okay...I like you too," I said as a smile was plastered onto my face.

HIs head snapped in my direction as the ends of his mouth began to twist upwards into a grin.

"Really?" He asked in disbelief.

"Yeah, I just don't want to take it too far because we are a few years away from finding our mates, it would complicate things," I frowned.

Gloominess washed over Avon's face as he looked away.

I got up from the ground and swung my leg over his waist so that I was now straddling him as he looked up at me with shock and blushed. I lowered my head down so that our lips were touching ever so slightly and I smiled.

"Or we can just not tell anyone and have some fun," I grinned mischievously.

It felt as though the ground under me had disappeared and I began falling to my doom. I realized a door had appeared right under me and opened without my command. I landed inside a building to see a woman screaming in my younger self's face.

"Oh my Goddess he's your mate?!' The woman screamed excitedly.

She was a beautiful woman that had similar features to the young girls except her eyes were hazel and her complexion was a bit lighter. There was a man standing next to her with a tired look in his eyes, much older than the woman next to him with a more chocolate complexion, a grin was plastered on his face.

So these were my parents.

"yes yes Mom I already assumed he would be my mate," A teenage Ava rolled her eyes.

"Don't catch an attitude with your mother young lady," My father growled.

"I'm gonna reject him," I rolled my eyes.

"You will do no such thing!" My mother screeched.

"I can't be with someone I don't love, we are complete opposites and it just won't work," I explained, by the look in my eyes it seemed as though I was trying to cover for something, that the words I were saying weren't truly what I meant in my heart. But what was I covering for?

"But you were just telling him a few months ago that you loved him and you hoped you both were mates," Her father said confused.

"I cheated on him and he broke up with me cause I met some people he didn't like, we just don't want each other anymore," I shrugged my shoulders.

My mother's face began to grow hot with anger as she grabbed the younger Ava and pulled her out of the room.

I processed the memory that had just gone down before me. So Avon wasn't just some childhood friend, he was my mate when I was mortal, it seemed as though I was guarding something and choosing to hold back what I really wanted to say but what if I was right? Was a really a cheater? Have I really lived all of my lives being scared to commit to men? Was I truly a bad person?

A new door appeared before me as I reached out with hesitation.

As I walked through there appeared tree and a dark figure laying on the ground as they bled out motionless. I walked over to get a closer look and realized it was a very naked me, flinching and shaking.

"Avangeline!" I heard a husky voice call behind me.

I turned around to see a tall muscular figure run over and bend down to check on the status of me.

"Avangeline it's me, Avon," he whispered to me.

I screamed at the sound of my name as I curled up into a ball, intensely shaking in pain. Immediately he picked up my naked body and carried me bridal style to the pack house. As I followed behind closely and approached the pack house I heard Avon quickly call for the Alpha and the Luna.

Soon enough the Alpha and Luna came running out in their bed attire with frightened expressions on their faces as they noticed me in his arms.

"What happened?!" My father boomed out.

"Hunters," Was all Avon said before he rushed me to the pack hospital.

From the last few memories I've seen of Avon, to say he grew a little was a bit of an understatement. He grew much taller and his voice much deeper as the muscles bulging around his body made him seem bigger but I couldn't get rid of that innocent look in his baby blue eyes, a look that seemed so precious to me.

My mother came running through the halls screaming my name.

"Avangeline!"

Each time she screamed my name the more and more my screams and shakes became worse and worse.

"Luna stop screaming her name!" Avon shouted.

She immediately shut up as she flopped onto the floor holding her head in her hands.

"Luna it's going to be okay," Avon said as he comforted her.

She looked up at him teary eyed.

"Why did you come back to her?" She asked.

"I never left and she never rejected me, I love her too much to let her go that easily. She my everything, she's the reason I think life is worth living and she couldn't stay away from me even if she wanted to. She lied to protect me because she got into some trouble with the wrong people and now she's paid the price," He frowned.

The doctor walked out of Ava's room and bowed to the Luna.

"Luna I have some terrible news," He sighed as he started.

"Hunters may have gotten to her because it appears she has been tortured with a dangerous and lethal amount of wolfsbane. I...I'm afraid that her wolf spirit is no longer with us due to the amount of torture she has endured, it's a miracle that she was able to live on her own but the hunters may have mentally scarred her from being able to tolerate her own name without expecting some form of pain," The doctor explained.

Evangeline came running through the hospital and stopped when she saw Avon and her mother at my door.

The Luna shook her head as Eve fell to the ground crying.

I can feel her pain. Her wolf is gone and I know because my wolf calls out in pain for her but theirs no response, she's really gone," Eve cried out.

After a few minutes everyone walked into Ava's room and there I was, my younger self staring up at the ceiling as I laid down in the hospital bed with a hollow expression.

"I got too close to humans, I exposed who I was and they sold me to hunters, I didn't want anyone to follow after me if I disappeared so I lied, I lied about Avon. I couldn't let anyone else get hurt. They did unspeakable things to me, chained me from a ceiling, beat me, cut me open, whipped me, injected me with things as they frequently called my name until I couldn't take it," I said in such a monotonous voice.

"It's gone, everything is gone. I'm nothing but a human," I said as a tear escaped from my eye.

"Avangeline," Eva whispered.

"DON'T SAY MY NAME!" I screeched as I banged my and on the table, everyone watching as it began to turn purple and green from impact.

Another door appeared next to me and I quickly walked through it.

Fire and bloody bodies covered the land as buildings were up in flames as young children and people ran around screaming and crying, trying to escape with their lives.

"Mommy! Daddy!" I heard a scream.

I ran over and noticed myself around a small fire, clutching the Alpha and Luna dead bodies as I held them closer to me.

"Ava come on it's not safe here any more I'm sorry!" Avon pulled on my arm.

Tears clouded my vision as we ran through the woods but stopped at a body just before us, naked.

Eve was staring up into the starry sky while laying in a pool of her own blood, nothing but emptiness in her eyes.

"No no no no," I continued to shake my head as I looked down at Eve, dropping to the ground and clutching her body close to my chest.

"Ava please come, I can't go on without you," Avon pleaded.

I gently placed a kiss on Eve forehead as I closed her eyes to rest, she died righting for what she loved and now it felt like I was abandoning her.

We zipped through the forest, Avon pulling me along and careful not to go too fast since I had the mobility of a normal human when all of a sudden I heard gun fire.

Avon turned around as he looked down at me with fearful eyes until he realized I was alright, at that moment he eased up and collapsed.

I watched as I fell to the ground screaming as I clutched Avon as tight as I could, he looked up at her with starry eyes, trying to find his voice to say something but ultimately failing as the light began to fade from his eyes, truly leaving her alone forever.

"Avon please no not you too! Please get up!" I begged out as I screamed.

"The poor little mutt seemed to lose her mutt partner," A harsh voice said above me.

"Leave me alone!" I cried out as I clutched onto Avon's dead body tighter.

"How much do you think she would sell for?"

"LEt's find out, it has to be a pretty penny,"

I watched as 4 dark figures advanced towards me and grabbed me as they began dragging me away as I tried to fight for my life and failed.

Another door appeared right in front of me, this time much different than the others and as I walked through the door I was greeted by nothing but brightness as a younger me stood in front of me with a saddened expression.

"I'm so sorry my child," The younger me said.

Only this wasn't me, this was my Divine Moon Goddess projecting as whatever you needed to see most and in this case, I needed to see myself the most, and give myself a hug. She didn't have a true form, only a form that you were most comfortable with.

"I have pushed you beyond your limits and I have broken you down but soon it shall all end. Everything has a purpose and soon your purpose will be with the one you are destined to be with, do not let the past come back to haunt you but instead tackle it and create a brighter future," She said to me.

"I know now where all this pain comes from and it's hard not to harbor it," I said as I clutched my chest.

"Show everyone how you can overcome your pain and not let it control you, show them the reason why you are currently the only black winged assassin," She paused for a moment.

"When you and your partner finally mate you will have a strong urge to take his life because in his mortal form he cannot be mated to you so you must take his life out of love. Something you didn't do for Liam, he is alive and he is currently at the white wolf pack along with you, he is an archangel of the worse kind who is cursed because you took his life out of hatred and anger so now he shall roam the Underworld forever cursed," She explained.

"So what do I do now?"

She smiled at me.

"Go back,"

She blew in my face and I immediately opened my eyes as I sat up from the bed, gasping for air. I clutched onto to my body and realized this was the real world, I was no longer in my mind.

'He is alive and currently at the white wolf pack along with you'

I jumped out of the bed, no questions asked as I raced to the door and noticed Derek in wolf form as Liam was about to charge at me.

I screamed at the top of my lungs, one that shook the tree tops, sent the birds flying and caused everyone to cover their ears in pain as I raced forward and kicking Liam out of the way as anger began to consume me.

"You shall no longer have control over my mind or my life," I said as I outstretched my wings.

Chapter 23.

A va POV

I watched as he looked up at me with wide eyes from the ground, pure shock since it's been a few decades since he last seen me.

"Ava you're awake, what happened?" Eve asked surprised.

"Yes Avangeline, what did happen?" Liam smirked as he picked himself up from the ground.

"I think I should be asking you the same thing. You like a little stressed since the last time I saw you dear MATE," I growled.

It was true, his eyes were a much darker green than what they once were, he had dark bags under his eyes as his face slightly aged over the years as it seemed much colder and darker.

"That's what time will do to you, and a sword to the fucking chest," He smirked at me.

He eyed my giant black wings as he snorted.

"Nice upgrade but in my eyes you're still weak and useless like you've always been," His smiled dropped from his face as he looked at me menacingly.

My bow and arrow appeared in my hand as my eyes began to glow to lock onto my target and I raised them in the air, threatening him.

"Try me," I smiled.

He smirked and immediately launched himself at me, tackling me to the ground. I kicked me off me as I punched him in the stomach causing him to stagger back and give me room to attack him.

As he stepped away from me I took this as as advantage and shot an arrow directly into his left eye.

"You fucking bitch!!!" He screamed as he back straight into Zachary's arm's, groaning in pain.

Zachary placed him in a headlock, holding him still as I walked up to him and punched him straight in the mouth.

"You don't deserve to fucking be alive you bastard!" I screamed at him.

He looked up at me and spit his black blood into my face as I grimaced in disgust.

To humans Archangels meant power but to us, Archangels were evil beings who belonged in the Underworld where they could cause rampage in the lands, away from others. They no longer need blood to survive so due to the climate of the Underworld it causes their blood to turn black.

I wiped at my face with the back of my hand as I glared at him, smashing his dirty blood into his face as I smeared it around.

"You think you're so tough now but you're really not, you're still weak," He smirked.

I was no longer afraid of him. He no longer had any control of me, my mind or my body, the memories of him began to fade as I realized they were only memories and I was a much more powerful being than before.

"No, you're the weak one," I smirked.

"We'll see about that," He said.

Suddenly black smoke began to protrude from his hands as it quickly began to crowd the area, it was so thick as it quickly spread it became difficult to even breath. It was an uncomfortable suffocation that messed with your minds as your lungs screamed for air.

Just when I couldn't take anymore I extended my wings and flapped them forcefully against the smoke causing all of it to whisk away and for the area to become more clear.

I looked down and noticed Zachary laying on the ground with a cut on his arm.

"What happened?" I asked as I ran up to him.

"He attacked us all as he distracted us. He's much faster and stronger than we thought he would be," He groaned.

I noticed the scar began to heat up and slowly blacken, becoming a permanent scar forever. Archangels were one of extremely few beings that could permanently scar or even kill an Angel.

I heard a whining behind me so I turned around and noticed Derek's wolf laying on the ground bleeding out with a large gash on his neck.

I quickly ran over to him as I knelt down, a gnawing fear in my stomach as I approached him.

"Derek hold on, don't move!" I screamed.

He let out a heavy breath as he rolled his eyes at me.

"Eve! I don't know what to do!" I cried out.

"Ava he obviously has white wolf blood in him, see if you can heal him," She said.

I mentally face palmed myself as I looked down at Derek and pressed my hands firmly against his wound. Warmth began to ignite from my fingers as my eyes began to glow a bright gold, transferring heat to his wound. Within minutes later I removed my hands and noticed the wound was fully healed.

I sighed in relief.

Derek your wolf spirit is healed but your human form might be damaged, you'll need to be like this for a while,"

He nodded his head and rested his giant wolf head in my lap.

"Derek I'm sorry," I said as I petted his head.

He whined and looked up at me, tilting his head.

"I don't speak dog," I giggled.

He growled at me as I laughed.

"Well aren't you two just adorable," Ariel said as she stalked her way over.

Out of the corner of my eye I noticed Nicholas staring at us as he was attempting to compose himself, a pained expression was slapped on his face, making me feel sorry for him.

"If you ever need a real man Ava, you know how to find me," Ariel winked.

Derek looked up at me with a confused expression.

"I dunno, she has like a crush on e or something," I shrugged my shoulders as I smiled.

"Alright you two, we need to start discussing strategy and how Liam ended up being an Archangel," Eve said seriously.

"Could we actually do that a little later? I have something important I need to discuss with Derek," I said nervously.

"No Ava, this IS really important. We have no idea when Liam will be back so we need to think about-" I cut her off in the middle of her sentence as I shook my head.

"The Moon Goddess spoke these words to me and I need to relay them," I said.

She studied me for a moment before nodding her head at us and then walking towards the pack house.

"I need to tell you something in private." I said to Derek as I patted his head.

He sent me a little howl as he nodded toward his back. He was beckoning me to ride on his back.

Since he was larger than most werewolves due to the fact that he had Alpha blood and white wolf blood in him it wouldn't be a problem for me to ride on it. I hopped onto his back and the minute I clung onto his fur he took off running into the woods.

A small pond came into clearing view and he abruptly stopped as he growled, signaling for me to get off of his back.

I got off his back and sat next to him as he scratched his ear.

"Derek I found out what happens to you once we mate," I sighed.

I looked at him and noticed he tilted as if curious.

"I have to...um take your life in order for us to be together," I said hesitantly.

He rose up from the ground as he growled at me, until he was right on top of me and from there I heard bones cracking and shifting when I realized he was shifting right in front of me.

I looked away because it actually was a disgusting sight to see.

I turned back to notice Derek in his human form...naked and staring at me.

"Wow you heal really quick, I wasn't expecting you to shift back until another few days," I said as I chuckled nervously.

"What can I say, I'm extraordinary. Now run that back of what you just said," He said with a serious expression plastered on his face.

"I was told by the Moon Goddess that once we mate I will have a sudden urge to take your life and that is what has to happen in order for us to be together. The reason that Liam is an Archangel now is because I took his life out of anger and hate, with you it must be love," I whispered.

"Stand up," He said as he stood up himself and outstretched his hand to help me up.

I hesitantly grabbed it and the moment I stood in front of him he lightly cupped my face with both hands and smiled.

"Make sure you look me in the eyes when you stab me in the heart," Derek smirked as he pulled me in closer before kissing me ever so gently on my lips. There was so much emotions behind this kiss it made me want to melt underneath him but unfortunately I couldn't savor this moment long because there was a scream coming from the pack house that seemed to fill the entire forest.

Chapter 24.

Derek and I raced back to the pack in full speed and as we raced into the pack house I was stopped by Lucie who was looking at me with fear full in her eyes.

"Ava you have to help Nicholas! I don't know what's wrong with him!" Lucie cried out.

"Where is he?" I asked quickly.

"He's in his room but-"

I immediately dashed up the steps, not bothering to listen to what Lucie had to say because all I cared about was making sure that Nicholas was alright. I burst through his room door on the third to notice him standing by the window as he stared out of it, not acknowledging me.

"Hello Avangeline," He said without even looking at me.

I couldn't help but flinch at the sound of my name, a constant reminder of just how cruel my past life once was, something that would take a while to program out of my mind.

Nicholas what's wrong? Are you alright?" I asked, trying to ignore the fact that he just said my full name and he knew I hated that.

"Oh I'm not fine Ava, there's a pain in my heart that I can't get rid of until I do this, Avangeline I love you so much and it pains me to see you with that piece of shit Alpha. The Moon Goddess fucked up but now I'm gonna make things right," He growled as he advanced towards me.

I wasn't sure what was happening because Nicholas was never violent unless absolutely necessary so right now this was a bit off putting.

I tried to reach for the door but Nicholas slammed it shut as he glared at me with anger and jealousy, something I completely wasn't used to seeing from him and I didn't like this side.

Was this my wrong doing? Is this what I created by toying with this mans heart when I knew this was the wrong thing to do?

He grabbed me by my neck as he slammed me against the wall with such sudden strength but I knew for a fact he wasn't himself.

I clawed at his hand, trying not hurt hurt him but I just couldn't break free.

"Nic, th-this isn't y-ou!" I choked out.

He looked at me with desperation in his eyes as he grabbed my hands and pinned them above my head and buried his nose deep into the crook of my neck.

"You are mine and only mine," He whispered before I felt him sink his canines into the flesh of my neck.

It felt as though my heart would explode any minute from the pain as the blood painfully rushed to my head and my body became weak and fatigued, so this was exactly how Derek felt when Taylor marked him without his permission, it was so nauseatingly painful I almost couldn't bare it.

I screamed and pushed Nicholas away from me before racing down and out of the pack house before I could do anything to hurt him. I looked around and noticed Derek struggling to pick himself up from the ground as he clutched onto his head and looked up at me with such betrayal and hurt in his eyes.

"What the fuck Ava you let him mark you?" He asked out in annoyance.

"Derek I didn't want this! There's something wrong with Nicholas but I can't figure out what, he went hostile and decided to attack me," I tried to explain as I ran up to him.

"Fuck karma is a bitch," He muttered to himself as he rubbed his neck.

A silver arrow appeared in my hand and I lit the tip on fire, holding it dangerously close to my neck.

"What's going o-" Eve froze as she walked outside and noticed me with an arrow in my hands.

"Avangeline think about this first," Derek said as he slowly stood up.

I flinched as I nearly burned myself, everything was going fine but Nicholas just had to go and set us back.

"Ava put the arrow down now...wait who's mark is that?" Eve asked curiously as she looked at my neck.

"Nicholas marked me without consent and I want it off now!" I hissed.

"Ava if you do that then Nicholas is guaranteed to die, we have to figure something else out," She said slowly.

Nicholas came out of the pack house clutching his head in pain, the moment he got close enough to Eve she turned around and punched him square in the face.

He fell onto the ground and growled up at Eve as he held his nose.

"Why the fuck did you mark my sister when she already has a mate?!" She screamed.

"Because she is mine and mine only," He growled darkly.

As Nicholas talked I noticed his eye color was no longer his normal eye color, they were a strange dark grey, almost like Liam's color.

I whisked away the arrow and I briskly walked over towards him to help him up, he gladly took my hand but before he knew it I grabbed his head and pressed my thumbs against his temples as my eyes began to glow gold. I looked deep into his mind and noticed his thoughts were clouded with the thick dark smoke from earlier, rupturing his mind and creating thoughts that were no longer his.

The work of Liam.

I tilted his head as he struggled under my grip and blew hard into his ear, allowing for all of the smoke to trail out of his ears and his normal baby blue eyes to return to their former glory. As I finally let him go he collapsed to the ground and began vomiting a black substance until he was dry heaving.

"What the hell was that?" Eve asked.

"The smoke from Liam must have affected his brain somehow, sad to say that isn't enough to remove this mark," I said sadly.

Taylor quickly ran over to Nicholas as she helped him up on his feet, bringing him into a bear up as he stood up, him slowly returning the hug.

"Alright well today has been eventual and we can't just leave the white wolf pack while Liam is still on the loose, it's going to be a full moon tonight," Eve said.

Both Nicholas's and Taylor's eyes widened at the sound of the full moon.

"What's wrong with the full moon?" I asked, wondering if they were trying to disrespect the Moon Goddess.

"Mates who haven't mated yet give off a very strong and irresistible smell to each other, it's almost impossible not to fuck each other," Derek said as he approached me, smirking.

That would make perfect sense coming from the Moon Goddess, her origins of her being a hopeless romantic who wanted nothing more than people to find their soul mates were true before she sacrificed herself to become the Moon Goddess.

"Fine, to make things less messy and complicated Ava and I can share a room and Taylor and Alpha Derek can share a room," Zachary insisted.

Simultaneously Derek, Nicholas and I all growled at the same time.

"Ava isn't sharing a room with you," Derek growled.

"She's not sharing a room with Derek," Nicholas and I argued at the same time.

I looked over at him in surprise as he sighed.

"After marking you and you clearing my head of that smoke I truly began to realize your feelings for me...you never wanted me Ava and it was childish of me to ever think that I had a chance with you when all I've been doing was hurting the one I was destined to be with, I guess me and Taylor need to exchange some words," He chuckled sadly.

With the mark that Nicholas placed upon me he was able to understand my thoughts and feelings so instead of it bringing us together it would be the cause of us tearing apart.

"I think we all need to have a few words with our mates before the Moon Goddess tries to bind us together,"

Chapter 25.

"So what happened?" Eva asked as she looked down at me.

We were currently still in the white wolf pack but this time inside of a guest room as I was laying on the bed, contemplating a few things. Eve was also in the room taking precautions, locking up the windows and doors, wrapping chains around all of them.

"What happened where?" I asked as I rolled onto my stomach, cuddling into a pillow.

"You know, inside your mind," She said as chains appeared on the walls.

I wanted her to chain me to the wall because I couldn't risk any distractions after tonight, I needed to locate Liam and send him back to where he belonged.

"Oh just a few memories of my mortal self, we were pretty adorable when we were younger, an old mate, actually how you died, why I hate my name so much andtakingDerek'slife," I quickly jumbled the last part together.

"I'm sorry what was that last part?" Eve asked as she turned to me with her arms crossed.

I sighed.

"The reason I want to stay away fromDerek during the full moon tonight because the Moon Goddess herself informed me that once we mate I will have a strong urge to want to take his life because while he is a mortal werewolf he cannot be my mate," I explained.

"Damn I just thought you were into some kinky shit, have you told him yet?" She asked.

"Yeah, he knows,"

"Well I guess all the more reason to stick knives into you if you try to break out," She grinned at me.

I rolled my eyes as I looked I looked out of the chain covered window to see the sun setting, giving off an orange and pinkish glow.

It was quite beautiful.

"I wanna go see Derek," I finally admitted after a few moments of silence.

"Girl what did I just say? Plus it's almost night time and I chained up the door already," She whined.

"Please Eve, you can even come with me and keep watch," I pleaded.

"Alright fine just shut up," She huffed as she began unlocking the door.

As soon as she unlocked the door we noticed Ariel hovering down the hall with chains in her hands.

"Hey do you know what room Derek is in?" I shouted out.

Ariel slightly jumped as she dropped all of the chains and turned around with a furious expression.

"Don't fucking do that!" She yelled out.

"Sorry," I said innocently.

"I was just going to his room, come on," She beckoned for me to follow her as she picked the chains back up.

"I'm not leaving, Ariel make sure they don't get into anything," Eve called out from the room.

I followed Ariel down the hall and up a flight of stairs and we made our way to the end of the hall.

As we entered the room we noticed Derek laying on top of the bed shirtless, just staring up at the ceiling and I couldn't help but admire his physique as he laid there so peaceful.

"Hey I got the chains you wanted and if you really wanted to get freaky I brought your mate with me as an added bonus," She said as she dropped the chains to the ground.

He looked up from the bed with a annoyed expression.

"I thought you wanted to stay away from me?" He questioned.

""I have until the full moon is in full effect I'm fine," I shrugged.

"Get out," He said.

"Look I really need to talk to you, you don't have to be a-"

"I was talking about the other one that's floating," He pointed to Ariel.

"Alright well I'll be waiting outside so I can chain you up, sounds kinda kinky doesn't it?" Ariel winked at me.

"Just get out Ariel," I giggled at her.

She smirked and closed the door behind her leaving the two of us finally alone.

I eyed him for a while as he continued to lay on the bed until he finally sat up and looked at me with amusement on his face.

"Are you done gawking at me or should I wait to speak?" He chuckled.

I looked at him with a confused expression.

"Those aren't your shorts are they?" I asked.

"No I assume they are Alpha Nicholas's but I'm not sure. I destroyed my last pair of clean shorts," He shrugged his shoulders.

"So you're just wearing some random pair of shorts you found in here?"

""Yeah, they were clean," He said whilst stretching.

"So then whose underwear are you wearing? Another random pair?" I asked amused.

He paused for a moment before standing up and walking towards me. As he walked closer forward I began walking backwards until I felt my back hit the wall. His hand rested on the wall next to my face as he leaned in closer and smiled.

"And who said I was wearing any?" He smirked.

My face grew hot with embarrassment as I tried to look anywhere but down, he backed away from me, laughing, as his laughter boomed throughout the room.

Such a childish man but that was what he normally did, teased me, toyed with me and playing childish little games, it was actually a breath of fresh air and a break of the usual murder I had to do.

"You're disgusting," I joked.

"It was still pretty funny," He grinned.

"Well I didn't come in here to question you about underwear, I came to question you about something serious that determines our relationship," I said seriously.

HIs grin soon turned into a frown as he looked away.

"Guess I should have known this was coming," He sighed.

I felt a heat in my body that was beginning to spread but it was more of a tingly annoying heat instead of a pain so I decided to ignore it.

"Why did you have to go and kill my Elizabeth?" I asked.

He looked into my eyes with a look of endearment almost.

"It happened that morning you didn't come back, I had went out for a morning walk to see if maybe I could find you and explain to you what happened with Taylor and I which nothing happened at all, she started to take her clothes off in my office and try to have sex with me so I pinned her to desk a bit aggressively trying to get her to stop. I didn't know what was happening but I felt something jump onto my back as it sunk it's teeth into me and immediately I felt dizzy as if the world was spinning around me, I didn't know what was attacking me I just felt it biting me and clawing at me everywhere and the last thing that I did was call for the first person I could think of through the mind link, I woke up in the hospital banged up and I was told it was a vampire attack," He explained apologetically.

"Of course it would be fucking Taylor to take away what I love most," I growled.

"Ava I know from the moment I met you I haven't been the best mate or even person to you and you for a fact don't deserve me at all, for fucks sake you are THE black winged Assassin Angel that I've only heard about through stories. I never thought I would meet you let alone become your mate. I just want you to know from here on out I am all for you and whatever happens after you kill me I will always be by your side," He said as he approached me.

"Why don't you get on your knees and beg, men are so much hotter when they beg," I joked as I snickered.

To my surprise he quickly dropped to his knees as he wrapped his hands around my legs and sent a quick kiss to my inner thigh causing my heart to skip a beat.

"Like this?" He asked up to me as lust began to fill his eyes.

My heart was pounding madly inside of me as the heat began to spread more and more throughout my body as an enormous itch that couldn't be scratched.

"How can I prove to you that from now on I am for you and only you?" He said as his hands began to trail up and around my back, massaging every inch of my skin.

"Fuck Derek I don't know about this," I groaned, trying not to give in to the sensations.

I felt myself slipping in and out as my nose was filled with such an incredible smell, it almost calmed my senses but it just wasn't enough.

"I know you feel it Ava," I heard Derek say.

I looked down and noticed Derek staring up at me with eyes going in and out of black, his wolf on the verge of taking over.

"Yes it won't go away," I whined as I grabbed his arm to pull him up and hold him closer.

But it wasn't enough.

"I don't know how much longer I'll be able to control myself Ava, my wolf and I want you badly," He groaned as I noticed the pain in his eyes as he tried to hold himself back.

The heat inside of me was traveling rapidly and his scent helped ease it slightly but I couldn't afford for distractions right now, not in the middle of getting rid of Liam.

....Fuck this.

I grabbed ahold of Derek and roughly pinned him onto the bed with me straddling him. I reached down and kissed him with such hunger and passion that he immediately responded with equal hunger as me. It slightly alleviated the pain but it just wasn't enough, I needed more.

I felt his grip increase on my waist as his tongue gently grazed my bottom lip, I did what he wanted and allowed for his tongue to gently slip in. I gripped his muscular arms as I moaned into his mouth.

I heard the door slam open abruptly causing me to fall off of Derek.

"Avangeline get away from him!" I heard a scream behind me.

I flinched and suddenly felt a strong pair of arms swoop me up and hold me against his chest.

I looked up to see Derek looking furious as his chest rumbled as he growled.

"Alpha Derek just let her go," I heard Zachary say.

"No! She's mine and I will complete this process!" He growled, his wolf fully taking over.

"Ava come here!" Eve yelled.

I held onto Derek tighter and looked at Eve angrily.

"He's the only one that will make this pain go away," I groaned in pain.

"Don't make me tell you again," Eve yelled.

A larger growl erupted from inside of Derek.

I felt a sharp pain pierce my lower back as I pulled away from Derek. I landed on the floor roughly as Eve reached down to pull out a chain with a dagger attached to it.

Derek roared loudly as he advanced in our direction. Ariel and Zachary grabbed both of his arms and pushed him against the wall the restrain him. Eve grabbed and pulled me out of the room, I struggled around to get away from her grasp as she pulled me down the steps. I felt a sharp pain pierce my side as I noticed a dagger sticking out of it.

"I'll stick it in further if you don't stop struggling," Eve warned.

That only made me want to fight more.

Finally we reached my room where Eve threw me into, I collapsed onto a wall where all of a sudden tree roots burst through the wall, pinning me down as I tried to break free but the roots were too strong.

"Ava we gotta ride this out until the moon goes away," Eve huffed as she crossed her arms.

The intense heat was building more and more it was nearly unbearable.

"Eve please I need him," I begged.

She shook her head as she looked away from me.

All of a sudden there was a pained howl that echoed all throughout the house, the howl gave me sudden strength to break free from the restraints and glared up at Eve.

How dare she stop me from mating with what's mine.

Chapter 26.

It was like his scent followed me everywhere I go, filling my brain and drowning out my senses. It was as if the entire house was covered in nothing but his scent, teasing me, toying with me.

It was as if something else was controlling me, I was no longer in control of myself, all I thought about was mating with Derek, nothing more and nothing less.

But as much as I wanted this I had to fight this, I had to look at the bigger picture, I had to remember that there was a bigger objective to deal with.

Eve tackled me as we both landed on the ground with Eve on top of me.

"Ava if what you say is true then you can't risk this!" She shouted at me.

"I don't care what I said, Eve I need him please," I pleaded.

She shook her head as she remained on top of me. Sensations throughout my body began to fill so extreme and unbearable I knew I had to act fast.

I outstretched my wings I wrapped them around both Eve and I.

"Ava what are you doing?" Eve shrieked.

I stood up and opened my wings as a strong wing gushed from them, knocking Eve away from me. There was another howl coming from Derek's room, this time much more urgent and desperate. I dashed down the hall and up the stairs and burst through the door where Derek was being held down by chains, Ariel and Zachary.

I ran over and grabbed Zachary and Ariel to toss them aside. Derek got up and tried to walk towards me but the chains restricted him from doing so.

"Ava get away from-"

I raised my hand and both Ariel and Zachary were sent flying out of the room. I stood in front of the door and put up a protective shield so that no one else would be allowed to enter. Zachary, Ariel and Eve all came running towards the door but were immediately stopped by the barrier. They banged on it, trying desperately to enter but couldn't do so.

"Ava don't do this," Eve pleaded with me as she looked me in the eyes.

I smirked as I grabbed for the door.

"Too late," I slammed the door shut.

Eve's POV

"Well there's no stopping those two now," Ariel shrugged as she floated away.

"I didn't know the mate pull during the full moon could be that strong," I said, shaking my head.

I walked down the stairs and headed straight outside, looking up at the full moon and admiring it.

The moon was big and bright compared to the vast darkness surrounding it.

"Why were we even stopping them in the first place?" Zachary questioned as he walked up to me.

"Apparently once they mate Ava will have a strong urge to kill him in order for them to remain mates," I explained.

"I don't understand the whole gist of it but I guess there's nothing left to do now," Zachary said calmly.

I looked at him with confusion. He was taking this rather calmly than I was expecting him to be.

"Why are you looking at me like that?" He asked annoyed.

"Well asshole, I was just wondering why you were taking this so calmly," I hissed.

"What's done is done, she will always be attracted to her mate and I will always be a phase that Ava has gone through, all I can do now is stay out of the way and cause no drama," He said a bit sadly.

I almost felt sorry for Zachary. Almost, but some things just aren't meant to be.

I looked away and began walking towards the forest to be alone with my own thoughts.

What would happen when Ava and Derek finally mate? Would he become an Angel? Would she abandon me? She wouldn't just do that she's my sister, but would I be able to third wheel around with my sister and her mate? Would he become a higher rank than me?

Without realizing, I was walking deeper and deeper into the forest and that's when something grabbed my face and immediately I was bolted upwards into the sky. I tried to struggle against the grip so I could free myself but the grasp was just too strong.

Suddenly I was dropped.

I felt myself falling out of the sky and before I could even react I was landing face first, hitting the ground with many bones in my face breaking and painfully re healing.

"Fuck!" I yelled out, feeling the effects of the healing.

"I thought you were supposed to be a lot tougher than that Evangeline," I heard a husky voice say as it sent shivers down my spine.

I stood up, staggering a bit and looked up to see Liam looking down at me with his bat like wings outstretched.

"Are you trying to kidnap me?" I asked as I shuddered.

He swooped down from the tree he was perched in and landed right in front of me. Even in the dark he was still cold and intimidating as he was in the light.

"You're going to help me with someone or else I can do things to hurt you," He chuckled as he smiled at me.

I wasn't sure why I was quivering in fear so much. When Ava told stories about him I always imagined myself giving him a slow and painful death.

Now that he was an Archangel and up close and personal with me he honestly scared the shit out of me.

"And if I decide not to?" I said with shaky confidence in my voice.

He stared at me for a second with such a dark look as he chuckled.

"Have you ever encountered an Archangel Evangeline? You know there are only a few things out there that can actually kill you pitiful Angels," He smirked.

He raised his hand and gently caressed my face causing me to shudder in disgust.

"And what is that?" I asked.

He turned away from me, looking into the dark forest around us.

"Archangels are one of the only few beings that can potentially kill Angels, crush your souls until there's nothing left but the memory of you which is why you will help me or else," He turned to look at me with such a deranged look.

"I don't care if you take my life, it would mean the world to me if I am finally untied with the Moon Goddess herself," I laughed.

He growled as he leaned closer, his face dangerously close to mine and smiled.

"I know your weak spot Evangeline. What about that sister of yours? Avangeline, do you think she feels the same way?" He chuckled.

"You won't touch her!" I yelled.

He grabbed me and slammed me against a nearby boulder.

"Then you will simply do as I say," He growled.

"Never," I spat in his face.

A silver dagger appeared in my hand and I quickly sliced at his face causing him to yell and drop me. My wings sprouted from my back a I attempted to fly off, Liam grabbed my wings and threw me hard against the boulder until I was out cold.

"I'm out for her blood," Was all I heard before darkness surround me.

"Eve!"

"Evangeline!"

"Eve wake up!!!"

I bolted up and noticed Nicholas and Taylor staring at me and based off their worried expressions, that meant something wasn't right.

"What's wrong?" I asked as I lifted myself from the ground.

I flinched as I looked behind my back and noticed my wing was broken.

"Eve, your wing is-"

"Let's not worry about me right now, what's wrong?" I asked impatiently.

"Alpha Derek is in a frenzy," Taylor said.

I looked at her as I rolled my eyes.

"Last time he was in a frenzy you attempted to have sex with him, just go get Ava to calm him down,"

Nicholas growled at me.

"That's not the point right now Eve, every time Ava comes near him her eyes go black and she tries to attack him,"

I jumped up and tried to fly up into the air but I was sent crashing down as pain overtook my body from my broken wing.

"Eve just follow us, obviously you can't fly right now," Nicholas beckoned for me to follow them.

We walked throughout the forest and I noticed Nicholas and Taylor walking side by side, talking amongst themselves.

I continued to stay silent as I walked behind them, as soon as the pack came into view I heard screaming and yelling coming from the house. I ran ahead of the couple and burst through the doors revealing a black eyed Ava holding her sword in her hand with Ariel holding her back with vines and Alpha Derek being held back by Zachary, eyes as dark as night.

"What is going on?" I screamed over the loudness.

"She tried to kill him!" Ariel shouted.

Chapter 27

Ava POV

I felt something soft and warm peppering the mark around my neck and I couldn't help but moan softly. Mating under the full moon allowed for the marks of Nicholas and Taylor to fade away and allowed for one another to rightfully mark under the full Moon, something the Moon Goddess predicted for I expected.

I heard a soft chuckle behind me and I knew it was Derek.

"I know you're up," He said as he began rubbing my arm. I kept my eyes closed and pretended to sleep but truthfully I was wide awake.

"Ava I can hear your thoughts, I know you're not sleeping," He chuckled.

Damn it, I wasn't used to this mate connection.

I heard that.

I groaned as I buried my face into the pillow.

" I don't want to get up. The others will lecture me about what happened last night," I groaned.

I remembered why they were holding me back last night, but I didn't have the urge to kill Derek so maybe the Moon Goddess was wrong.

"What happened last night was natural and you shouldn't be ashamed of it," He tried to reassure me.

After a few moments of silence I felt him remove the covers from my naked body and slap my ass as hard as he could.

"Time to get up!" He said, with a chipper attitude.

I immediately shot up and glared at him but what I saw scared me.

I should have known the Moon Goddess makes no mistake.

Derek was glowing, not in a healthy natural way but his skin was glowing bright red as voices began to chant things in my head as I continued to stare at him.

He's mortal

Kill him

Sacrifice his mortal life

He will be reborn

Be together forever

Kill him

My thoughts were not my own as I looked at him and before I could feel myself slip, I closed my eyes and laid back down.

"Ava what's wrong, that face you gave me was a look of fear," I heard Derek's worried tone.

I shook my head as I kept my eyes closed.

I felt him grab my face as he pulled me up.

"Look at me please and tell me you are okay," He pleaded.

My eyes shot wide open and all I could see was Derek glowing before me. I felt a silver dagger appear into my hand with command as the voices in my head continued to grow louder and louder as my eyes grew darker. It was as if I no longer had any control over my body as I slashed at Derek's face but he quickly moved out of the way.

What are you doing, what's wrong?" He asked as he moved away from me.

"We have to be together forever," I said in a monotonous voice as I lunged at him.

"Fuck I didn't think it would happen so quick! Ava I have to appoint a new Alpha of my pack before I allow you to kill me, the moment isn't right," He shouted.

My bow and arrow appeared in my hand and I quickly fired.

The arrow lightly grazed his skin and caused him to hiss in pain.

I ran up to him and pinned him against the wall but Derek was a fighter and he knew how to get out of situations like this. He forcefully kicked me in the stomach sending me flying into the opposite wall.

The door flew open revealing Ariel, Taylor, Zachary and Nicholas. Derek growled angrily at Zachary and Nicholas as if signaling for them to leave.

I took this as a chance and lunged at Derek in full speed but he grabbed me and threw me straight into the wall.

"Ava you have you stop!" He yelled at me.

"What the hell is going on?!" Ariel asked.

"She's trying to kill me!" Derek growled.

'Well then get out!" Ariel yelled as she rolled her eyes.

Derek quickly dashed out of the door and immediately felt myself calming down but at the same time I was missing his presence.

"Alright Ava come on and put some clothes on, you're naked and fighting Derek so it's a weird view. Not that I'm complaining or anything," Ariel chuckled.

I quickly rushed on my clothes and looked over to see Ariel gawking at me with such an amused expression.

"You know you have a great body, just the whole package," She winked.

I rolled my eyes as I headed down the stairs to discuss finding Liam.

'Ava I want to see you again'

Derek I miss your touch

'And I miss yours, please come to me'

I whimpered at Derek pleading in my mind. I walked down the stairs until I was in the living area where I noticed Zachary and Nicholas staring at Derek with concern. He was looking out of the window at who knows what but I knew what exactly he was thinking about.

He was thinking about me and thinking about death, wondering what's going to happen after he truly allows for me to take his life.

"Ava come here," I heard his husky tone.

I quickly closed my eyes and slowly began walking forward but not careful enough. I trip over something and as I quickly braced myself for impact but instead of falling on the cold hard ground I fell into warm hard hands.

I felt the sudden urge to open my eyes and caress his face but I kept my eyes shut.

"I wish I could see your beautiful brown eyes," He whispered into my ear and pulled me into a tight embrace.

I shivered at his breath and nearly opened my eyes.

"Derek you can't say things like that. I want to see your face so bad but I can't risk it, I need to remain focused," I said sadly.

"When this is all over, you're mine and no one else's," He whispered.

Crazy how much of a sensitive little shit I've become for this man in just a few weeks.

Derek chuckled.

"How do you think I feel? I never imagined I'd be so infatuated with someone in a matter of weeks,"

I made the wrong mistake by opening my eyes. For a second I forgot our differences and the circumstances we were currently in and most of all I forgot that he couldn't be fully mine until I officially took care of Liam.

I opened my eyes and noticed Derek looking at me with shock as my eyes grew darker.

Kill him.

Kill him.

He will finally be yours.

My celestial sword appeared in my hand and simultaneously there was a scream as I was jerked backwards, away from Derek.

I looked back and noticed Ariel holding me back with vines sprouting from the walls and I looked over at my target and noticed he was being held back by Zachary.

"Let her go!" Derek roared.

"I'm saving your life dumbass, just think!" Ariel yelled.

I tried to reach back and cut away the vines but she restricted my hands.

"Ava don't do this, you don't need a distraction while trying to find Liam!" Zachary shouted as he struggled.

Eva burst through the door with a broken wing and he looked at all of us.

"What the hell is going on?!" She shouted.

"She tried to kill him!" Ariel shouted.

Chapter 28.

"Ava please stop you can't do this, I have to tell you something important!" Eva shouted.

"It can wait!" I snapped as I turned to her.

I stared long and hard at her broken wing and that was when I considered hearing what she had to say.

"Please take him away from me, I can't control myself around him," I sighed as the vines began to loosen their grip around me.

I heard struggling for a bit until I heard Derek finally say "I can handle myself," He growled.

As soon as I knew he walked away I looked up and looked at Eve.

"What's wrong, what happened to your wing?" I asked immediately.

"Last night Liam found me and attempted to get him to help me with something or else he would hurt you. I said no and he slammed me against a boulder which broke my wing and it surprisingly didn't heal. Listen Liam is out for your blood and he knows that Derek is your mate so he knows your weak spot and he will use it against you," Eve explained and pleaded.

I felt myself growing hotter and angrier by the minute. How dare Liam attack my sister just to come after me, if he wanted he knows he better come straight to me.

"We need to track him down now, I don't care what it takes we just need to find him before it gets to us. Zachary and Ariel I need you to bring Derek back to his pack, he needs to clear a few things up before he can fully join us," I ordered.

"Ava we are we going to do?" Eve asked me.

I looked her dead in her eyes and smirked.

"We are going to train,"

"Ava I can't train with a broken wing," She rolled her eyes.

"Well it's not going to heal because you didn't snap it back into place, technically the boulder broke your wing and not him so it should heal," I walked over to her and grabbed her wing as she hissed in pain.

"Count to three and I'll snap it back into place," I said.

She nodded her head as she flinched.

"One..."

I grabbed her wing and immediately snapped the joint back into place. She screamed out in pain and back away from me.

"You said count to three!" She screamed at me.

I grinned at her mischievously,

"You would have expected it,"

"Alright so what's going with you and Derek?" She asked.

I sighed.

"I can't help myself, every time I see him I want to murder him but not because I hate him, because I love him and I want him to be with me forever,"

"Forever sounds like a lot of sex, hope you know a bunch of positions to try," She giggled.

I glared at her.

"You're not being serious, this isn't just about sex Eva," I scolded.

"By the way you were throwing us around just to get to Alpha Derek seemed like sex is a major part of the package," She giggled.

I groaned and turned away from her.

"Speaking of package, would you care to share how big-"

"Evangeline! Now is not the time to ask such questions!" I shouted as I covered my ears.

'Talking about me to your sister?' I heard his snarky voice in my head.

No, she's just asking uncomfortable questions about you.

'Why don't you answer then? Is it too much for her to handle?'

I growled out loud my accident causing Eve to look at me weirdly.

"I'm sorry I was talking to Derek," I said.

Watch what you say out of your mouth Derek.

"Ava come on, Ariel and Zachary went back with Derek so let's go train now since my wing is healed," Eve said, pulling my arm.

I followed her outside and watched as she placed a protective shield around us.

"Now remember Ava, give your best shot, I won't die so hit me like you would hit Liam,"

At the moment she said that I immediately punched her straight in the jaw. She staggered backwards and grabbed her jaw before looking up at me and smirking.

"That wasn't your hardest hit, you need a little motivation," She said.

"I won't be able to give you my all unless Liam is standing directly in front of me," I rolled my eyes.

She thought for a moment and I watched as she began to grow taller and her physical features change and before I knew it I looked up to see Liam staring down at me smirking.

"How about this? Does this make you want to rip my throat out?" Eve asked in Liam's deep tone.

I huffed loudly and pulled out my bow and arrows.

I knew it was my sister just trying to bring. out my inner beast but whenever I looked at her in this form I saw that horrible monster I wanted nothing more to get rid of.

"Give me your all," She smirked.

I sent an arrow whizzing towards her but she quickly dodged out of the way.

She raced towards me and pulled out her silver knives, I quickly smacked her away with my wings sending her flying into the shield. She landed on her feet and glared at me.

Silver knives began to appear in her hands as she began launching them at me lightening speed. I tried to block most of them but they began cutting away at my skin.

I flapped my giant black wings at her causing a gush of wind to speed towards her, she jumped out of the way and landed behind me. Before I could react, she wrapped her giant bat like wings around me, crushing me. I felt trapped and crushed, I knew if this was actually Liam he would kill me instantly. I pulled out a knife and cut straight through the skin between the wings.

She pushed me away from her and let out a giant screech like a bat. I opened my mouth and a stream of fire came rushing out towards her til she was knocked backwards against the dome and struggled to get up. I rushed forward, towards her and held a blade up to her neck.

Just as I was about to finish the job I heard voices in my head and visions began to appear in my mind.

I saw a fuzzy image of Ariel and Zachary walking in front, frustrated.

'Is Ava alright?' I recognized it as Derek's voice in my head.

Shit, I didn't mean to enter into his mind right now. I felt something push hard onto my stomach and I was sent flying against the dome. I felt my spine shatter and repair painfully.

I landed on the ground and cracked a few ribs which also healed painfully.

Eve walked up to me, still in Liam form and smirked.

She flipped me around and straddled me while holding a knife to my heart.

"You have to do something about Derek, He is a distraction that could easily get you killed," She said.

There was a loud screech and I watched as the entire protective shield shattered around us. Eve was yanked away from me as I sat up to see a tall man in shite slacks, no shirt and no shoes. He had extremely long blonde hair down to his back and blacked eyes as his white wings spread out.

Within the Angel assassins, wing color determines your rank but Angels throughout all worlds are ranked by the symbol burned into your chest over your heart.

Right now the symbol burnt onto this Angel's chest was a pair of giant bat like wings on a giant gate.

He was a Guardian of the Underworld.

Chapter 29

I ran up to the guardian and yanked him off of Eve until he was sent flying backwards. He landed on his feet and glared at me. Just as he was about to attack my I raised my large black wings so they were visible to everyone and ripped away at the color of my shirt revealing the symbol of a sword crossing a pair of Angel wings. The symbol of the assassins, something that we all had.

"My apologies, Alatum sicarius," I looked down to see him on one knee bowing.

There were different obligations when it came to becoming an Angel, servant, messenger, guardian, protectors, Angels of nature, Angels of Death, Angels of life but Assassination happened to be one of the top rankings because it required a level of skill since no mortal or immortal was safe from us. It was a dangerous job that only few could handle.

"Why are you not guarding the gates of the Underworld?" I asked.

He rose rose from his position and looked at me with his stormy black eyes. They say you could see the entrance of the the Underworld from the eyes of a Guardian.

"Alatum Sicarius, I was looking for this one," He pointed towards Eve. Eve got up and looked at herself as she realized she was still in Liam's form. She shook her head and slowly began to shift back to her original form.

"It seems I was mistaken, shape shifters are a rare phenomenon amongst Angels so I didn't bother to check, I apologize," He said as he bowed.

"She was helping me train that's all, the one you are looking for is named Liam and he's incredibly strong and powerful so we will need your help," I said.

"Alatum Sicarius, I'm-"

"Just call me Ava please, the formal names are a bit annoying don't you think? Come inside and I will explain things to you," I beckoned him to follow me.

"Ava? I don't need your help," He said, staying exactly where he was.

I looked back at him and raised my eyebrow.

"I don't care whether or not you need my help, it is my task to destroy Liam, a monster I created so COME INSIDE," I hissed the last part.

He hesitated before walking into the house after me. We walked inside and the noticed the guardian looking around at the interior, as if fascinated.

"What's your name?" I asked him.

"Lucas is what I can be referred to as," He said.

"Well Lucas want to let me know how that asshole escaped from the Underworld?" I growled.

He looked at me with a blank expression on his face.

"I'm sorry but that information is classified," Lucas said.

"Listen Lucas, you better have a plan on catching this guy because he ruined her life and she deserves some justice, I don't give a shit if you wanna work alone, this Angel is the highest ranking and closest to the moon goddess and you will work with her to stop this son of a bitch," Eva shouted.

Lucas looked at me and turned his head to the side. "All I want is to comprehend the fugitive Archangel, if we can do this without disruptions then I guess I can work with you,"

"Don't worry, all distractions are gone now where do we start?" I asked.

"Tracking him won't be an option, we have to make him come to us," Lucas said.

"And how do we do-" Eva started to say before I smacked her.

"He wants me dead and I know Liam accepts a challenge no matter what. Maybe I could challenge him and he would have no choice but to come here," I said excitedly.

"Do you have anyone close to you?"

I paused and immediately thought of Derek.

'I don't like you being around another male'

'Derek are you back at your pack?'

'Ava I just said I don't want you being around another male'

'Derek please he is only helping me with Liam, I need to make sure your safe so no one will go after you'

'Ava I'm back at the pack discussing some things, just please be safe or I will find you and protect you'

"Ava!" I jolted up and noticed Lucas and Eva staring at me.

"Are you alright? You kind of went blank for a second," Eva asked.

"Ava I- is this a bad time?" Nicholas walked in with Taylor by his side.

"yes this could be a bad time," I shrugged.

"What are mortals doing here? They could be in danger," Lucas said coldly.

"This is the white wolf pack, heavily guarded by the Angels and moon goddess herself," Nicholas snapped back.

Lucas walked up and spat in his face.

"You are still mortals, do not get it confused for you are no where near as connected to the Moon Goddess as us," Lucas said warningly.

Nicholas growled and approached Lucas.

"Watch what you say out your mouth, before I have to put you in your place," He growled.

"And my place is above you, looking down at you in your poor mortal form," Lucas smirked.

I stood in between them and placed my hand on Lucas chest.

"Tanti non est retro," (Back down he is not worth it) I said as I shook my head.

Eva shook her head at me and walked out the door.

"Everyone's a damn drama Queen," I heard her say.

"Nicholas this is Lucas, he is the Guardian Angel of the Underworld and isn't really used to being around mortals, he's only helping me with Liam," I said to Nicholas.

"You don't need help from this joke, you can take Liam yourself, he'll just be in the way," Nicholas growled.

"Nicholas stop! I need you to make sure all of your pack members say inside the house at all times and to never come out, this could be dangerous," I grabbed his arm.

Taylor approached me and growled as she noticed me gripping Nicholas arm.

"Taylor I'm not in the mood to argue with you, this isn't the first time I touched what's yours just like you've touched what's mine now drop it," I hissed at her.

"Avan-" there was a scream outside that could be heard all throughout the house.

We all immediately stopped and ran outside to see Liam standing on top of Eve, ripping her beautiful white wings out from her back.

She was below his feet, laying on her stomach as Liam ripped her wings right out of her back, blood praying everywhere.

"EVE!!!!!" I screamed as Liam picked her up and threw her into the forest. My wings sprouted out of my back as I dashed toward her to catch her football style. I grabbed her and landed on my back into the forest so she that get harmed anymore that she has already.

"Eve are you okay?" I asked her. Her eyes were closed and her face was scratched up and didn't look like it was going to heal as empty bloody sockets in her back continued to bleed out, showing no signs of healing. Her face was slowly losing color as her hair that was once purple was now turning back to her natural color of black.

"No, no no Eve stay with me!" I shouted.

I gripped onto her hand and felt her tug on my hand slightly.

"Ava, damn it hurts," Eva whispered as she lightly chuckled.

"Evangeline what hurts? What hurts?!" I cried out.

She turned to her side and I noticed a sharp piece of Liam wing stuck in her side. Her skin began turning black around it and I noticed she was bleeding out.

She was losing too much blood without healing.

I yanked it out of her side and felt her flinch. Her skin was so pale it was turning a grayish color.

"They say when an Angel dies, another will be reborn," She chuckled. "Just never thought I would be that Angel to die,"

Her weak grip released my hand and flopped to the ground as her eyes showed a vacant expression.

"Avangeline," Was the last thing she said before she looked straight up into the sky and the light disappeared from her eyes.

Her body began to form a giant white light as it ascended into the sky and past the clouds.

Now she left me with nothing.

I stood up with my knees shaking with anger. How dare he take my sister from me. How dare he come back into my life, taking everyone away from me.

I walked out of the forest still shaking with anger, I felt my body heating up and my eyes turning red. He doesn't deserve to get shot with an arrow. He deserves to get his head cut off with my sword.

I walked out and noticed Liam pinning Lucas down on the ground with him struggling.

I ran forward and threw Liam off of him.

"You've taken everything from me, I have nothing now because of you, you're not going back to the underworld Liam. I'm going to fucking kill you," I said warningly.

"You still have that dear mate Avangeline, I'm gonna make you take his life and watch the light slip from his eyes and then I'm taking you with me," He smirked.

I pulled out my sword and watched the sun reflect off the silver I held it with two hands in front of me and steadied my footing.

"I'd like to see you try."

Chapter 30.

(The picture is Liam wings)

"I'd like to see you try."

Liam and I both ran toward each other as I raised my sword ready to strike me. He kicked me straight into the chest and sent me flying backwards into a tree.

"Ava!" I saw Nicholas and Taylor running towards me. I blew hard in their direction causing a powerful wind to knock them backwards into the forest, safe from harms way. I got up from the ground and picked up my sword.

Lucas ran towards me and looked at me as if asking for answers.

"Fly up and attack from the sky, I'll distract him on the ground," He nodded and rocketed into the sky.

"Oh Avangeline! We aren't done yet darling! I'm gonna break you!" Liam laughed as he walked towards me.

I looked up at him and screamed as flames shot from my mouth straight toward him. He covered himself with his wings so I ran up to him and sliced at his wing. The skin between the joints were sliced open as he screeched out in pain. Flaming chains appeared in his hand as he lashed out at my arms. I hissed in pain and whisked away my sword. I kicked him in the knee causing him to fall on his knees and punched him square in the nose.

I looked down down at the scars on my arms and noticed they were turning black. As soon as I looked up, something connected to my face causing me to fall backwards.

I landed on my back and groaned.

Liam looked down at me and smiled as his black blood dripped from his nose and onto my face.

"Your not special, your wings are black and bigger so what? You have no real power,"

I rolled over to my side and smacked him with my wing. He landed on the ground but quickly got up as I got up.

"That's where your wrong Liam I-" I felt a sharp pain in my side. I noticed he lashed my side with his burning chains.

Note to self, never make any speeches about strength while in the middle of a battle.

He lashed out again but this time I caught the chain and twisted it out of his hand. My arms and hands began turning black like coal to adjust to the flames just as his did. He looked at me with amazement as I begun spinning around in a circle full speed. Soon all around me was a giant flaming tornado with me and the chains in the center of it, shredding anything in its path. I started advancing toward Liam. As he tried to fly away, I caught his wings in the tornado and began shredding them with the chains excruciatingly. He screeched out in pain as I shredded his wings and lashed at him body. I felt warm hands clasp around throat as I stopped what I was doing to try to get the hands off of me.

He banged my head on the ground and removed one hand from my throat only to punch my in the face with full force.

"I will punch your face in until you're screaming out in pain," He threatened as he continued to punch me. Blood was leaking down my face, bruises were forming and my eye was becoming more swollen.

He raised his fist and smirked at me.

"Remember this love? Every night I would beat you and apologize and you would just fall for it!" He laughed.

I raised my head a little and spat my blood in his face. Just as his fist was about to come down to my face again he gave out a loud bat like screech and got off me to grab something to throw it at me.

Instinctively, I caught it and growled when I realized what it was. Derek looked at me in wolf formed and whimpered as he noticed my face.

"Derek get out of here!" I shouted at him.

He ignored me and charged at Liam who was staggering around due to the bite mark Derek gave him in his leg. He knocked him off his feet and began snapping at his face.

Where the hell did Lucas go? Did he abandon me?

A whimper and whine snapped me out of my thoughts as I noticed Liam stuck Derek in the leg with a dagger.

I ran forward and kicked Liam straight in the chest. I knelt down to Derek who was panting hard and laying down on his side. He looked at me with a pleasing look as if saying just end it.

"Just do it Avangeline," I flinched at my name.

"Do it or I swear I will murder him horribly in front of you," Liam growled.

A silver dagger appeared in my hand as I felt the urge consuming me and taking over.

"I love you," I whispered to Derek.

I stuck the knife straight into his chest and watched as he became motionless, he began shifting back to his human self. I knew I was destined to do this but it pained me to see his lifeless body staring up at me with no light, no twinkle in his eyes.

I clutched his body and let the silent tears slide down my face as I realized how much love I had for this man. My moment was quickly ruined my Liam dragging me away by my hair. I screamed and clawed at his hands until he let me go and kicked me in my face.

He bent down to my face and growled.

"You're mine now bi-" before he could finish, I opened my mouth and screamed as flames shot out of my mouth straight towards his face. It pained my throat but it was worth watching Liam scream and cover his now burned face.

He let go of his face and chains appeared in his hands. He lashed them out, capturing my hands. As I struggled he began pulling the chains, like his mission was to tear off my limbs.

Just as I thought it was the end, the chains disappeared and there was a loud screech behind me.

I looked behind me to see Lucas holding Liam in place as he squirmed around.

I stood up and walked toward him. Liam looked at me with shock across his face.

"Well I guess you're my bitch now," I smirked.

He continued to screech and struggle as my sword came into my hand. Without hesitation I stabbed him straight in the chest, piercing him straight through. At that same moment one of his hands got free and he stabbed me in the chest with something sharp. I flinched and fell to the ground as his body became motionless. His body began turning into a giant cloud of smoke as it created a giant hole in the earth and zoomed straight to the center. Lucas looked over at me and then back to the hole.

"Thanks," He was all he said before he dived straight into the hole and closed it up.

"Ava!" I heard a yell. I didn't have the strength to look up because it was draining out of my body.

Nicholas appeared in my view and yanked whatever was in my chest out. He held it up and I noticed it was a piece of the bone from Liam's wing.

I didn't know something so ugly could have such a terrible effect on you.

"No no no Ava you'll be fine stay awake, just stay awake," Nicholas pleaded.

"Nicky I can't, I'm so sleepy," I cried out. Tears slid down my face.

Looks like Derek would have to survive without me.

My eyes kids began to droop and it became increasingly harder to keep them open.

"No Ava I refuse for you to die in my arms right now," Nicholas warned.

I held his hand and smiled at him.

"Apparently this was destined to be, be happy with your true mate and live your life free from me finally," I smiled.

I grew weaker and weaker until I finally I would be one with the Moon Goddess.

There was a flash of light in the sky and the ground rumbled.

The last thing I could hear from Nicholas was

"Hurry up she's over here!"

Chapter 31.

(Picture is of the Angels weapons)

Beep beep beep

"Shut that the hell up!"

"Harder!"

"Come on man harder!"

"Shut up! I don't know what I'm doing!"

"Your eyes should be glowing and you should be healing her!"

"I'm gonna fucking kill you if you don't shut up!"

"You can't kill me! But you're gonna kill her if you don't concentrate,"

Beep beep beep

I opened my eyes to a bright light blinding me, I tried to sit up but a sharp pain took over my chest. As my eyes adjusted to the light I realized I was in a really large room with the windows open.

I looked up to see a door slowly opening to reveal Natasha. She looked up at me and smiled.

"Good you're awake, they weren't sure if you were going to wake or not," She said.

She opened the door fully and brought in a tray full of food.

"You know I'm immortal, I don't need to eat." I stated.

She shrugged and placed the tray in front of me.

"Food usually helps with the pain," She said as she handed me a mirror.

I looked through it and noticed my eye was no longer swollen, the bruises were gone but there was a long scar across my eye and a gash on my right cheek. I looked down at my arms and still noticed the black scars on my arms from the lashes.

"He healed most of the scars and bruises but some just wouldn't go away, he did the best he could," She smiled sadly.

I was so confused. Who healed my scars?

"Who are you talking about?" I asked.

"Alp-"

There was banging and crashing coming from outside of the door and yelling. There was a knock at the door but then the entire door fell off its hinges.

There stood a surprised Derek with giant black wings sprouting from his back.

"I didn't know that was going to happen," He muttered.

He stepped inside while struggling to fit his wings inside.

"Derek why don't you retract your wings?" I giggled.

"I don't know how, it feels like extra weight on my back," He muttered.

"Concentrate on your wings, you control them, imagine them retracting into your back or shifting like you would if you were shifting," I explained.

He closed his eyes and his wings began to shift into his back, he fell on all fours as he flinched from the pain until they were fully gone.

"You'll get used to the pain, just like shifting," I smiled.

"I'll leave you two alone," Natasha giggled.

Once she left the room, Derek brought me into a bone crushing hug. I returned the hug as silent tears escaped me.

"I missed you so much, I thought I was going to lose you," Derek whispered in my ear.

I laughed as I cried into his shoulder.

"Look at the Big Bad Alpha being sensitive," I laughed.

"Never discuss this with anyone." He growled into my ear before he smiled.

I lifted my head so I was looking him in the eyes and smashed my lips against his. He growled in satisfaction as he climbed on top of me. I wrapped my legs around his waist and smiled against his lips.

"So when I said sex forever, I didn't mean around me because I'm not interested in seeing live action, like you could have fixed the door at least," A familiar voice said in the doorway.

I looked past Derek's shoulder and noticed Eva standing in the doorway with a look of disgust on her face. I pushed Derek off of me and bolted towards Eva. I jumped on her which caused both of us to fall to the ground.

I began squealing and kissing her all over her face.

"Avangeline get off of me!" She screamed.

I flinched and automatically got off of her.

She quickly helped me up and apologized.

"I'm sorry Ava I keep forgetting that hurts you," She said.

"How are you here right now?" I asked excitedly.

"Ask your boyfriend here," She scolded.

Warm hands wrapped around my waist and I turned to see Derek looking down at me lovingly.

"How is she here right now?" I asked him.

"I dragged her back down here," He grinned.

I turned to Eva with a confused expression.

"We were both going through judgement, the Moon Goddess was quick to give him his wings, he saw me and literally dragged me back down here," She crossed her arms.

"Looks like you're stuck with me forever," I grinned.

She rolled her eyes and smiled.

"So what happened?" I asked.

"We came back down and noticed Taylor and Nicholas screaming about how you killed Liam and he stabbed you in the process, Derek remembered how you healed him and Ariel so he healed you, you were out for a few weeks," She explained.

"You still look beautiful with your battle scars," Derek whispered in my ear.

"So we are back at your pack?" I asked.

He nodded his head.

"It's not my pack anymore, I can't be an immortal running a wolf pack, I gave leadership to Daniel and Natasha, I told them to inform everyone I died or something,"

I took his hand and led him outside to the open field.

"Well what's your weapon?" I asked excitedly.

"Weapon?" He asked.

"Only black winged Angels can store multiple weapons, other Angels have one specific weapon, Eva's is daggers, Ariel likes to use nature. I prefer my bow and arrow," I said.

He closed his eyes and giant silver axes began appearing in his hands. He opened his eyes and amusement filled his eyes.

"Damn you look badass!" Eva said.

'Let's go flying'

I heard him say in my mind.

I nodded as he whisked away his weapons.

"Eva sorry to fly off but I gotta go," I said and rocketed off the ground.

Soon Derek caught up to me as we both enjoyed the breeze in our face and each other company.

Before I could react, something flew straight into me.

"Ava!!" It screamed as I steadied myself.

I looked up to see Ariel, Elijah and Zachary grinning at me.

"Welcome back from the dead," Elijah smiled.

"Good to be back," I grinned.

Eva flew up with us and smiled.

"Aww look at the most deadliest beings on the planet having a reunion in the sky." Eva awed.

Everyone laughed at Eva and smiled at each other.

"Derek, Ariel I'll race you guys," I smirked.

"Even if you two are black winged assassins I can still beat you." Ariel smirked.

"Alright, ready, set GO!" All three of us zoomed through the sky as fast as we could.

I guess the moon goddess was right when she said everything will turn out fine with me.

I have a loving mate, now 6 co workers and I am the most powerful Angel there is.

I am the Angel with the Black Assassin Wings.